TEASING THE DEVIL

MONICA BELLE

Published by Xcite Books Ltd – 2011

ISBN 9781908192721

Printed and bound in the UK

Cover design by The Design House

Chapter One

WE NEVER DID FIND out exactly why Julian d'Alveda was expelled. All we knew was that it had happened in the chapel, that it involved a girl from the village, and that it was, above all, dirty.

I pretended to be horrified, just like everyone else. Secretly I was thrilled, but then I always did have a taste for the darkness, and for Julian d'Alveda. He was older than me, very dark, with a strong, slightly harsh face that must have come from his Portuguese father and the blackest, deepest eyes I've ever seen. I used to watch him across the dining hall and imagine his powerful, bony hands on my body, doing things to me I'd never had done, rough things, rude things, things polite young ladies very definitely were not supposed to permit. His only failing, in my eyes, was that he seemed rather detached, academic, and far more likely to be found in the library with his nose in a book than out on the playing fields.

Then there was the scandal and any doubts I'd had disappeared completely. I was fascinated, entranced, my imagination running wild as I imagined what might have been going on when Reverend Smith caught them, and imagining myself in place of the girl. In the very tamest of my fantasies I was naked across the alter as he took me from behind, and the things I thought about in my wilder moments – late at night with my knickers pushed down and my hand busy between my thighs – those were enough to leave me blushing afterwards, for embarrassment at my

1

own dirty mind.

I knew I was safe, of course. He was gone, and he'd never taken the slightest notice of me anyway. Why would he? I was that much younger than him, shy, studious and a bit of a mouse, I suppose, with my glasses and my hair up in a bun, my outward image a million miles away from what was going on in my head. True, I did get quite a lot of attention to my figure, but not from Julian.

The scandal happened on midsummer night, not all that long before the end of the summer term. By the autumn we all had new things to think about, and Julian d'Alveda and his expulsion quickly passed into legend. I still thought about him, particularly late at night when the disturbing, arousing thoughts would begin to crowd into my head, but I had no idea what had happened to him and I wouldn't have had the courage to do anything about it if I had.

So time passed; my last few terms and my year off as a conservation volunteer in India, and university, to leave me a little wiser, a little more cynical. I'd almost forgotten about Julian as I sat in the careers room wondering what to do with myself. Term was over, campus almost deserted, myself and a few other unfortunates who were obliged to stay on beyond the end of term the only students about. The thought of settling into a regular job was depressing. I didn't feel in any great hurry to start an attempt to climb the corporate ladder, but I was skimming through magazines on the off chance of finding something to inspire me.

I was reading an article on unusual jobs and suddenly there he was, as darkly handsome as ever, with a group of people on a sunny lawn in front of a house built of flints and age-blackened wood. I was sure it was him, but had to check the text to make sure I wasn't fooling myself. Sure enough, he was showing people around Candle Street Hall in Norfolk, a tour guide for ghost hunters. I'd always imagined him being terribly successful; a politician

2

perhaps or a high-flying banker, with a trophy wife six feet tall and most of that leg. To see him doing something I might easily have aspired to myself gave me mixed feelings; sadness to see my idol fallen, a sudden thrill blended with remorse to think that perhaps he might have been accessible after all. I was also curious, and suddenly wistful, remembering how he had made me ache, how I'd wished he'd even notice me, how I used to touch myself over him in the warm comfort of my bedsit; my top up so that I could play with my breasts, my knickers off or taut between my ankles, my thighs spread to the summer darkness as I thought of myself in the chapel, made to do something at once utterly unspeakable and impossibly thrilling.

For maybe two months it had been my favourite fantasy, giving way only once I was on holiday and involved in the romance which had come to a climax with me losing my virginity. Yet even at that moment of glorious surrender my thoughts hadn't been entirely focused on the boy on top of me, and while my sigh as my body had filled for the first time in my life had been genuine ecstasy it had also held a trace of regret. I'd been ready for a while, and I'd wanted him to do it somewhere special, somewhere daring, at very least outdoors where we'd be at risk of getting caught, maybe in his car knowing that there might very well be a peeping Tom in the bushes, better still over the alter of the local church while the bells chimed midnight high above us. I got it in my own bed at the cottage my parents had rented in Wales, with my sister trying to stifle her giggles in the bunk above us. Still, it had definitely been rude, very rude.

I had to shake myself to clear my head, smiling ruefully as I pushed away the absurd thought which had popped up from nowhere, of how daring and how good it would be to misbehave right then and there, teasing myself to a climax in the careers room, when anybody might come in and

3

catch me at any moment. It was insane, impossible, a completely stupid thing to do, to risk having somebody catch me masturbating, and yet just the thought of it sent a powerful shiver down my spine. I suppose I'm a natural exhibitionist, but I'd never acted on my impulses and I wasn't about to start now.

Smiling for my own silly thoughts, I got up and went to make myself a coffee. It was amazing how Julian d'Alveda had got into my head, lifting me from utter boredom to a sharp, needy arousal in the space of a few seconds, as if he'd somehow put a spell on me. It was a ridiculous idea, because he hadn't even been there, but one of the many rumours after his expulsion was that he had been engaged in some sort of ritual, something to do with witchcraft or even Satanism.

The memory sent my thoughts down a new track. As I stood sipping my coffee I was imagining how it would be if he had somehow made his picture project a strong desire to any woman who saw it, or better still, just to me. If that was the case I'd be helpless, unable to stop myself. I'd start to tease my breasts, struggling to fight the urge but unable to stop my fingers as my nipples came up until they were sticking out, high and proud, making two very obvious little bumps in my top, little bumps nobody who came into the careers room could possibly fail to notice.

I wouldn't stop there, far from it. With every touch my arousal would grow stronger, and my helplessness. I'd be astonished at my own behaviour as I removed my bra under my top and tugged it all up to show off my bare breasts. He'd know too, somehow, amused and horny as I cupped my breasts, feeling their weight in my hands as I held them up to show off to him, his cock a hard bulge in his trousers as he appeared from nowhere, beckoning to me, cool and commanding as he told me to get on my knees and fold my flesh around him, and to suck his cock as well, to suck his cock while he fucked my cleavage.

4

Again I shook myself. The words alone were impossibly dirty; shocking, shameful, utterly inappropriate for any self-respecting woman, and yet utterly compelling. In ways they were worse than the act, although it was all too easy to imagine the horror of my friends if they caught me like that, on my knees to a man, his cock bobbing up and down between my breasts and I kissed and licked at the head. They'd call me a slut, tell me I was degrading myself, making myself the instrument of male sex fantasy. I'd be burning with shame, but I wouldn't be able to hold back.

I couldn't. My nipples were hard, the ache between my thighs was too strong to resist. I was going to do it, then and there. Nobody was about, the few students in college all out enjoying the bright summer sunshine. I'd be able to hear anybody who did approach anyway, the tiled floor of the corridor and the utter silence ensuring that I heard footsteps long before the door was pushed open to expose me. That was what I was telling myself as I tugged up my top anyway.

Just having my bra showing felt so naughty a sigh broke from my lips, and my fingers were shaking as they went to the catch behind my back. One hook, two hooks, and the catch came free. I felt the weight of my breasts loll forward, took hold of the cups, lifted and I was bare, topless, holding my own weight in my hands, satisfyingly full and heavy, my nipples painfully sensitive under my fingers. It felt so good, to be showing off in a public place, for all that I couldn't stop shaking or biting my lip with nervous tension.

A last flicker of common sense made me go and sit in a high-backed chair under the window, giving me the best chance of covering up if anybody did come and making sure nobody outside could possibly see me. With that went my last chance of holding back from utterly disgracing myself. My skirt came up, tugged high around my waist to sit the seat of my knickers on the coarse weave of the chair.

I gave a little wriggle, enjoying the feel of rough cloth on the flesh of my bottom and thighs. Another quick motion and my knickers were down, my bottom bare on the seat.

My thighs came open, stretching the little scrap of cotton tight between my knees. One arm went to my chest, supporting the weight of my breasts, one nipple taut between finger and thumb. My spare hand went between my legs and I was doing it, stroking and teasing as I shut my eyes and let my mouth come open in bliss. I let my thoughts drift, to my fantasy of being under Julian's spell, imagining it was for real, that I was helpless, unable to stop myself from masturbating in public.

His face came up in my mind, cool and handsome, his lips curled up in mild amusement as he watched me with my breasts bare and thighs spread, rubbing at myself in dirty abandon and unable to hold back. I thought of my friends watching, horrified, as Julian ordered me to my knees. He'd make me suck him erect. He'd fuck my cleavage. He'd come in my mouth and make me swallow, so that every single one of them could see.

That was too much. My back arched tight and I was gasping and mumbling his name, over and over as my climax rose up inside me to burst in my head, not just once, but again and again, shock after shock running through my body as I clutched at myself and my nails dug deep into the soft flesh of my breast. His name was still on my lips as I started to come down, dizzy with reaction and bittersweet yearning for what might have been.

Chapter Two

IT WAS ONLY AFTER disgracing myself in the careers room that I realised there was nothing to stop me visiting Candle Street Hall. The thought of seeing Julian again gave me butterflies so badly I felt a little sick, and I couldn't help but imagine a ridiculous scenario in which I introduced myself and he didn't even remember who I was. That seemed depressingly likely, but telling myself that I could go but not introduce myself seemed just plain silly. I kept trying to tell myself I was 23 and shouldn't be behaving like an adolescent, but I've never been good at rationalising away my feelings.

I decided not to go, yet booked a place on his ghost tour the same afternoon. The journey was only just over an hour by coach and bus, which dropped me in a sleepy Norfolk village outside a big brick and flint church almost completely hidden by trees. It was a hot, still day, the air full of summer scents and the lazy drone of insects, not creepy at all, which made the conversation of my fellow tourists seem very odd as we gathered at the lych gate. One or two tried to engage me in conversation, but I answered in monosyllables, unable to focus on anything but the arrival of Julian.

He was coming to collect us in person, that much I knew, but I hadn't expected him to step out from the churchyard as if appearing from nowhere. In the picture he'd been all in black, as he was now, but no photograph could have done justice to the reality. His plain, slightly worn top was tight over the smooth muscles of his chest and abdomen, his jeans looser but hinting at muscle beneath and an impressive bulge where it mattered the most. Just that would have been enough to make me look, never mind his dark, dark eyes and the set of his mouth, which seemed ever ready to twitch up into a half smile as if at some private joke. Everything about him exuded masculinity, confidence, also a touch of mystery, especially his voice when he spoke.

'Ladies, gentlemen, welcome to Candle Street Hall.'

I knew he was putting on a show for the tourists, but that did nothing to calm the fluttering in my stomach or prevent me hanging on to his every word as he made his introduction. He hadn't noticed me, but I was right at the back, behind a truly huge American in a Hawaiian-style shirt. I was hiding, and I knew it, but I didn't dare step out, unwilling to face the moment when he failed to recognise me.

Once he'd introduced himself he motioned us towards where the mouth of a lane emerged from between two giant oaks, still talking.

'You will excuse me, I am certain, if we make a slight detour on our way to the house. This is Black Dog Lane, along which, in 1749, the then verger of St Peter's, one John Aickman, was chased down by a gigantic black dog. He was found the next morning in the very lych gate under which you now stand, in a state of terror from which he never recovered. They reckoned him one of the lucky ones, for the hound was, or is, no mortal dog but an apparition said to be part of the Devil's own pack and known locally as ... Chloe Anthony?'

He was looking right at me, eye to eye, and I felt the blood rush to my face as the entire group turned to look at me, no doubt somewhat puzzled. Julian was a great deal cooler, recovering himself almost immediately.

'I do beg your pardon, ladies and gentlemen. I wasn't

expecting to see an old friend here today. The hell hound is known as Black Shuck, this young lady is Chloe Anthony.'

'Hi.'

The word came out so faintly I barely heard myself speak, but for all my embarrassment as the tour group greeted me I was singing inside. Not only had Julian d'Alveda recognised me, but seeing me had broken his legendary poise, if only for an instant, and he had called me his friend. I did my best to play it cool, explaining to the big American man and his wife that I'd been at college with Julian and claiming that I'd just happened to be passing through. He'd walked ahead, leading the group into the mouth of Black Dog Lane, but I was sure he could hear me. Candle Street wasn't on the way from anywhere to anywhere else, cut off by a loop of the River Yar. He'd know I was lying, maybe that it was him who'd drawn me there. I could even imagine that he knew exactly how I felt, and every little detail of the fantasies I'd built around him over the years.

Whatever he knew, or guessed, he wasn't showing it, once more his usual calm and collected self as he led us down Black Dog Lane and across a field path. The village had been on a slight rise, but the land beyond was absolutely flat, the lane running between great old oaks with a ditch to either side, following the gentle curve of the river until we reached a gate from which a footpath led arrow straight across the fields. Julian waited until we had all caught up before speaking again.

'And there, ladies and gentlemen, we have Candle Street Hall.'

I recognised it from the picture in the magazine; a long, two-storey house built of flints and age-blackened timbers, with high, eccentric gables and chimneys higher still. Like the village it was built on a slight rise and grown about with mature trees, so that it seemed to have its own private island among the wide, flat fields. It also projected an aura, not of menace exactly, but like something I hadn't felt since I was a little girl, when a group of boys had dared me and my sister to go into an abandoned house. At least, it seemed to, but Julian had been building it up as we walked, describing how each midsummer night the ghost of Lady Howard left the house in a coach made of bones and pulled by headless horses, so I wasn't sure if the aura was just suggestion.

We struck off across the fields, along the path and across bridges and duckboards where a piece of wetland fringed the rise. Julian explained that there had once been a moat and launched into another grisly tale, of how the original house had been besieged and sacked during the Civil War. He was good. I could almost see the flames and hear the screams of the family and their retainers as they were slaughtered, despite it being a bright summer day and as peaceful as could be. He carried on as we mounted a set of crooked stone steps leading up between the trees.

'And this is Mary's Stair, where Lady Howard would walk in the evenings while under house arrest. Imagine how she felt, when every day might bring pardon, or, as it eventually did, her nemesis.'

I found it easy, so easy that I as I turned to look back over the fields to where the tower of the church rose above the trees I felt a cold shiver. My companions were no less affected, some quiet, others talking in hushed voices as we came out from the trees. Julian continued to relate the history of the house, which certainly seemed to have had more than its share of macabre incidents, if nothing else.

There was something else. The moment we were inside, the atmosphere grew stronger – a lot stronger. Our surroundings were more or less as I'd expected; oak-panelled walls hung with portraits, including one of the unfortunate Lady Howard, a wooden staircase dark with age but highly polished, a carpet in tones of red, rich browns, old gold and black. That gave a sense of age, of decorum, but had nothing to do with the sensation of dread rapidly building within me. Only Julian's presence kept me from running back out, and that he was trying to hide a grin. I caught the word "creepy" from one of my companions and Julian began again.

'And well it might be. Not only are we where Lady Howard collapsed when they came to take her, but she appears as the Grey Lady on the stairs. It is said that sensitive people can feel the emanations of her fear and despair.'

I could, although I've never been superstitious and certainly never thought of myself as susceptible to weird feelings. So could the others, to judge by their reactions, of nervous silence or thrilled, frightened comments conveyed in whispers. As if we were in a cathedral, it didn't seem proper to speak loudly, if at all, but that didn't seem to bother Julian, who remained calm and easy as he began to answer our questions. I listened, taking it all in and trying to work out if he was playing some kind of trick on us. If so I couldn't figure it out, and as we began to ascend the stair the sensation grew stronger, until I could barely make myself go on. One of the other women in the group couldn't, but gave a sudden, stifled sob and dashed for the open door, where the sun was streaming in from the garden. Julian followed, and I realised that if he shut the door I was going to panic.

Nobody wanted to stay on the stairs, and we clattered down in a group. I wanted to go outside, but I couldn't help but try and impress Julian, so stayed in the hall. Everybody else left, and it took all my will power just to stand there, pretending to admire the pictures. I knew I could cope, just as long as that door stayed open, and I was hoping that Julian wouldn't notice I wasn't among the group gathered on the lawn and come back inside to make sure I was all right. He came, but he didn't look concerned in the slightest, more amused. A quick glance to make sure none

11

of the others could see us and his mouth broke into a loose, boyish grin.

'That was perfect! It's not often somebody breaks like that.'

I didn't answer, my feelings too strong and too mixed to find words at all easily, but he carried on anyway.

'You know how it works, don't you?'

'No. Have you set something up?'

'Not I. It's a natural effect, well, man-made but not intentional. What can you hear?'

'Um ... the others talking ... birdsong?'

'No, something else, something you hear all the time, something so familiar you don't notice it.'

'I'm not sure. It seems very quiet.'

'It is, but listen carefully and it's always there.'

'I don't know, some traffic I suppose ...'

'Exactly. Lady Howard died in 1712, but nobody noticed a strange atmosphere in the Hall until the 60s, which was when there was enough traffic on the A47 to set up a low-frequency vibration through the ground. That's why I run the tours late in the afternoon, during the Norwich rush hour. You can't hear it, but you can sense it, can't you?'

I nodded and he spread his hands, like a conjuror after a successful trick, smiling broadly as he went on. 'But never mind that. It's wonderful to see you. What are you doing here?'

'I ... I had no idea you'd be here. I just thought it would be interesting.'

I'd lied, clumsily, and I was blushing. He knew, the corner of his mouth once more twitching up into that familiar smile; amused, almost laughing. My face grew hotter still but he pretended not to notice.

'And is it interesting?'

'Yes. I thought it was real.'

'Everybody does, almost everybody, but look, I hardly

get to see anybody, living out here, other than endless tourists. You'll stay for a drink with me and talk over old times, won't you?'

At that moment two people from the tour group came back inside and Julian once more switched on his act, but I'd already nodded my acceptance. The tour continued, but I was walking on air, no longer affected by the weird atmosphere now that I knew there was a mundane explanation, but with my head full of surmise and also the most wonderful sense of self-worth. He was treating me as if I were an old friend, and an equal, not as the shy, mousy girl he'd barely so much as spoken to.

The rest of the tour passed me by completely, although he certainly impressed the others. By the end, when he finally ushered us back out onto the lawn they were chattering in low, excited voices, even those who'd been sceptical at first now convinced that Candle Street Hall was well and truly haunted. Most openly, even proudly, admitted their belief in the ghosts, and one woman even claimed she'd seen something from the corner of her eye as we left the library. Julian played his part perfectly, never contradicting anyone, but never actually lying either, although he only talked for a couple of minutes before excusing himself and giving them the freedom of the grounds.

He went indoors and I followed. In the kitchen he poured out large glasses of chilled white wine. Now I knew what to do, to let him lead and hope it was towards bed, or if he didn't, to take over the role of seducer myself. Knowing Julian, and from the way he kept looking at me, I was sure that wouldn't be necessary. I was ready too, ready to be taken from behind over the kitchen table, and if the entire tour group came in and caught us, well, I'd always wanted to be watched. He was cooler, a little, because I was sure the bulge in his trousers was larger than before.

'So what have you been doing?'

13

'Oh, this and that. I've just finished uni.'

'Where?'

'Ipswich. And you?'

'Here and there, this and that.'

I'd been hoping he'd tell me about his expulsion, but for all his calm, friendly tone I could tell that he didn't want to talk. Nor did I, unless it was something to set my imagination stirring, and as he moved a little closer I made no attempt to back away. He read me perfectly, his fingers settling on the curve of my hip, an intimate caress, but not too intimate. I looked down, my cheeks hot and my fingers shaking as I put my glass on the table. He reached out, tilted up my chin and I was looking into his dark, dark eyes, melting as his lips met mine, my mouth opening to his, our tongues meeting as he took me in his arms.

That kiss sent my need high, so high that any last flicker of resistance just vanished. His arms were around me, holding me close into him, his big hands at the nape of my neck and in the small of my back, stroking at my skin through the light summer dress I'd chosen so carefully that morning. His teasing fingers moved lower, to the swell of my bottom, but I only cuddled tighter, too turned on to think of the need to preserve my dignity by not making myself too easy.

Again he got the message, cupping my cheeks in his hand and fumbling at my dress as his other hand went to my chest and his mouth left mine to move to my neck. I closed my eyes, lost to what he was doing to me, delighting in the way he was taking advantage, so rude, so urgent. After all, I'd imagined the moment a thousand times, and this was no time to play the lady.

I let him pull the straps of my dress off my shoulders and tug the front down even as I was exposed behind. My knickers were on show to the window as he eased down my bra, spilling my breast into his face. His lips found my nipple as his hand pushed into the back of my knickers,

14

taking them halfway down. My mouth came wide in a long sigh and I was lost, not just to the beautiful sensation of his touch, but also to the picture of how I would look should anybody chance to glance into the window; my clothes dishevelled, my face set in bliss as my half-naked body was explored. Most of all I was lost to him, because it wasn't merely an attractive man who was taking advantage of me so rudely, it was Julian d'Alveda.

He could have had me then and there. I'd have let him, and to hell with the consequences if we got caught. He had more control, teasing me until I could hold back no longer and my hand had found the swell of his cock beneath his trousers, but then pulling away. Nothing more needed to be said. He took my hand and led me to the corner, where a narrow staircase led up to the first floor. I was giggling, my chest still half bare, eager to be taken wherever he pleased and for whatever he wanted to do. He chose a bedroom, not the first we passed, which were all small and bare, but another, beyond a door and overlooking the hall. It was huge, with double windows and a high, high ceiling, but there didn't seem to be much space, because most of it was occupied by the most enormous bed I've ever seen.

Not that I was given time to admire the furnishings. He pushed me down and climbed onto me, my legs already wide and high by instinct. I could feel the bulge of his cock against my sex and took hold of him, my arms locked across the muscular width of his back, expecting him to simply unzip and push himself up me with my knickers pulled to one side. He didn't, but pushed himself up on his arms, leaving me hanging from his body for an instant before I let go. I was still helpless, trapped beneath his weight with my legs cocked wide, and more helpless still as he took hold of my wrists, holding both easily in one huge hand.

'What are you doing?'

'Something I've wanted to for years.'

As he spoke he'd taken hold of the front of my dress, to tug down the side that still covered me. I began to wriggle a bit, pleased by his attention and the rapt expression on his face as tugged my bra up to leave me with both breasts bare. A faint hiss escaped between his lips and he shook his head, his eyes locked to my chest, making me giggle.

'I'm not that big!'

'You're perfect.'

He ducked low, still holding my wrists, to keep me helpless as he began to nuzzle and kiss at my breasts. It tickled, in the nicest possible way, and the sense of being in his power was overwhelming, setting me wriggling and squirming beneath his body. He took no notice, enjoying my breasts as if it were the first and the last time he'd ever take pleasure in a woman's body, and all the while with the bulge pressing to my sex growing firmer and larger. When he finally stopped it was sudden, his voice coming with a sharp intake of breath as he released one now achingly stiff nipple from between his teeth.

'Perfect, so perfect! Just to have you bare ...'

His voice trailed off as he raised his body. One quick motion and my legs had been thrown up, another and my knickers were off, my bare sex now spread to his body. His hands went to his crotch and I realised I'd poked my tongue out to moisten my lips, a quite involuntary reaction as he drew down his zip. Out came his cock, thick and pale and already rock hard, just as big and beautiful and horny as I'd imagined it, only now rearing up over my open, ready pussy. I wanted to hold it, to suck it, to lick his balls and kiss his long white shaft in an ecstasy of worship, but all that was pushed aside by the sheer strength of my need.

'Put it in.'

He didn't need telling. Taking hold of himself he guided his cock to the mouth of my sex, watching as he did it, so rude, so open in his enjoyment of my body. I felt the pressure, and that glorious feeling of being opened by a man's cock, and filled as he slid himself in with one easy motion until his balls were pressed to the cheeks of my bottom. As he began to fuck me he stayed as he was, dark eyes half lidded and feasting on my bare chest as he eased himself in and out. For a moment the pleasure was simply too great to let me do anything but lie there and take it, but he was being rude with me and my dirty mind took over in seconds.

I began to play with my breasts, kneading them and tugging at my nipples, deliberately showing off what he obviously liked the most. He responded with a pleased purr and a smile, encouraging me to get ruder still, squeezing them together in my hands as I remembered how I'd come over the thought of him fucking my cleavage. At that he got faster, once more pushing my pleasure up too high to allow any control. I'd began to gasp and shake my head, still holding my breasts and desperate to please him. He pushed harder still, and faster, until I was wriggling on his cock and panting out my desire, utterly lost to what was being done to me.

That alone would have been glorious, even if it meant finishing myself off under sticky fingers once he was done. With most men that would have been it, but not with Julian d'Alveda. He knew he had me, and he took every advantage, but in ways I had no objection to whatsoever. Instead of simply coming inside me he pulled out his cock and began to rub himself on my sex, the firm flesh of the head bumping over my clitoris. He was watching too, a perfect, filthy detail as I lay back, my thighs rolled as high and wide as they would go, my breasts in my hands, showing him everything as he coolly, casually masturbated me to orgasm with the head of his cock.

When I came I screamed out loud, indifferent to who might hear and totally abandoned to him, just as dirty as I could possibly be with my belly thrust out and my bottom squirming on the bed as I struggled to get even more friction to my sex. He let me come, holding himself there until I'd finished, my ecstasy dying slowly until I'd finally let go of my breasts and spread my arms for a badly needed cuddle. He wasn't standing for any nonsense, his cock still rock hard as he adjusted my legs to climb over my body, his thighs now open above my waist to pin me helpless on the bed with his erection rearing above my breasts.

'Oh, you dirty ...'

He came, over my breasts and in my face, the perfect climax to our encounter because it was a moment I'd be masturbating over for ever. Only as he slowly settled a little of his weight onto my belly did he speak.

'I've wanted you so long, Chloe, and to do that ...'

I was smiling as he trailed off with a long, satisfied sigh, utterly relaxed, only to go rigid with shock as a figure stepped out from behind him – a woman; tall, dark haired, imperious, her handsome face set in an expression of amusement and disdain as she spoke.

'If you must bring your sluts back to the house, Julian, at least have the common sense to wait until the punters have left.'

Chapter Three

BEING CAUGHT HAVING SEX has always been one of my favourite fantasies, but the reality was very different. Maybe, just maybe, if she'd come in a little earlier, and if Julian had told me it was OK, then I'd have enjoyed what happened. After all, I'd been in a very, very dirty mood and as long as I knew she was enjoying the view I might have been all right.

As it was I was left speechless and red faced, so utterly overcome with embarrassment it was all I could do to make a completely hopeless attempt to cover myself up and then dash for the bathroom the moment Julian had climbed off me. Unfortunately I had no idea where the bathroom was, but assumed that such a gorgeous room would have an *en suite*, which is why I ended up in a cupboard full of old waterproofs, dressing gowns and assorted gents evening wear before Julian managed to rescue me.

He was pretty cool about it, too cool in fact, trying to laugh it all off as if nothing had happened and not even taking the woman to task for calling me a slut. It was only later that I discovered who she was – Vanessa Aylsham – the owner of Candle Street Hall, along with her husband. That was after I'd cleaned up, when she introduced herself, and while she wasn't actually nasty to me her voice was rich with both humour and utter contempt when she spoke. Even without that the memory of how she'd seen me would have been too much, and I left as soon as I possibly could, without even having a decent conversation with Julian.

I was in such a state on the bus that I couldn't think straight at all, and I only gradually began to calm down. Julian had said he hoped to see me again, and if we hadn't been caught I knew I'd have been singing, which did a lot to help me get the better of my embarrassment and shame. Once I was on the coach things didn't seem quite so awful, and I even managed to raise a smile for the thought of how unutterably rude I must have looked with my legs cocked wide and Julian mounted over my tummy as he finished himself off over my chest.

Another good thing was that I was sure she was jealous. That went some way to account for her attitude, and after all, there was no possible question that he was gorgeous. There was also no possible question that he wanted me, and had done for a long time. I'd never met a man who took quite so much delight in my body, and to judge from what he'd said he had been as keen on me as I had on him. Maybe he'd been flattering me, but his passion had been real, and if he'd never really paid attention when we'd known each other before that might have had more to do with my age than anything else.

By the time the coach was moving through the pretty Norfolk countryside I was really feeling quite good about the whole thing, despite an instant rush of blood to my cheeks every time I thought of how we'd been caught. I'd even begun to wonder if I could find some way of taking him up on his invitation, while avoiding Vanessa Aylsham. Possibly we could meet somewhere near the Hall, out in the country. There would be plenty of lonely spots where he could take me and handle me the way he had, with me pinned firmly to the ground and he enjoying my body, thoroughly using me and yet making very sure that I came too, and first.

I'd never really had a chance to come down, and the thought sent a strong shiver through me. At that my spirits finally began to lift. It didn't matter about Vanessa

Aylsham, for all my embarrassment. She was just jealous – and a stuck-up bitch at that. *I* was the one who'd been with Julian. *I* was the one who'd had rough, rude sex on what I now realised was probably her marital bed. *I* was the one who'd been in ecstasy, just as I would be again as soon as I was safely back in my room, or maybe before.

The coach had picked up speed, with the driver concentrating on the road and there were only half-a-dozen other passengers, all sitting well in front of where I'd put myself in the second-to-back row. The windows were high too, so high that unless a lorry or another bigger coach drew up beside us I couldn't possibly be seen. All I needed to do was lift my dress up at the front, slip a hand down my knickers and I'd be there in no time. It was tempting, very tempting indeed, but after what had happened before I couldn't make myself do it, for all that it seemed completely safe. I told myself that the coach was due to stop in Diss, and that we'd soon be there, but I'd have finished well before we arrived.

When we did I was half hoping that the coach would fill up, giving me an excuse not to be so dirty. It didn't, two people getting off in return for just one, and he chose to sit right at the front. I was biting my lip as we pulled away again, but every time I thought of Julian and how he'd handled me my muscles gave a little, sharp jerk. The moment we'd picked up speed again my skirt was up. I was soaking wet, which was no surprise, and just to touch myself brought my naughty feelings on so strong there was no going back.

As I began to stroke myself I was imagining that Julian was with me, his mouth set in that wry smile of his as he watched me masturbate. He'd order me to do it, enjoying my shame and the thrill of making me be dirty with myself as much as the sight of me with my skirt hauled up and the damp white triangle of my knickers on show as I stroked myself through the material. Yet that wouldn't be enough

21

for him. He'd want me bare, and he'd tell me to pull my knickers aside, no, to take them right off.

To think was to act. With trembling fingers I slipped my knickers down and off, stuffing them hastily into my bag before getting back to work. It wasn't going to take long, not long at all. I was rubbing eagerly, my clit a hard bump under my finger, the steady vibration of the engine an added thrill. Again I thought of Julian making me do it, and making me return the favour, bent down into the double seat with his lovely big cock in my mouth.

I hadn't sucked him, though I'd wanted to; I felt a sudden pang of regret even as my orgasm started to build. It was such a shame, when his cock was so perfectly suckable, and I'd only insisted we might still have been at it when Vanessa caught us. I'd have been on all fours, my bottom stuck up in the air and my knickers off to show her every single rude detail of my body as she came in, grabbed me by the hair, forced my head down on Julian's erection and held me firmly in place until he'd come in my mouth, calling me a slut as she forced me to drink down every last drop. It was a lovely climax, long and hard, but as I finally let myself go limp and hastily tugged my dress back down all my earlier shame came flooding back, for what I'd done and the way I'd been caught, but mainly for coming over the thought of the vicious bitch holding me by my hair as she made me swallow Julian's come.

It wasn't exactly the first time, more like the thousandth. I've always had a little kink in my brain which makes the most inappropriate things the most exciting, especially when I'm just about to come. Fantasising about Vanessa Aylsham being rough with me was really no different from 101 similar dirty details which had crept into my mind at the moment of orgasm. I've learnt to handle it, sort of, but there's no getting away from that first moment of hot shame when I've just given myself an orgasm over the thought of somebody being cruel to me, or unspeakably dirty with me, or humiliating me in some way, and more often than not it's another woman. Vanessa was a prime candidate too, with her knowing sneer and her money and her perfect but artificial beauty.

I did my best to put her out of my mind, but I wasn't giving up on Julian so easily. Back in Ipswich I immediately checked my email, but there was nothing and I didn't want to seem too eager, so I didn't send anything. I probably would have done the next day, because I've never been very good at playing hard to get, but real life gave me a nasty shock. My room was owned by the university and I knew full well I wouldn't be able to stay there for ever, but with no students coming up until well into September I'd hoped to spend the summer there, and even that they might forget to charge me any rent for the period.

The shock, the first shock anyway, was padding downstairs in my nightie and knickers just in time to meet a workman coming in at the front door. He was big, fleshy and completely bald, with a pair of little piggy eyes fixed firmly on my chest. I beat a hasty retreat, returned more decently clad to find five of them in the kitchen, where I learnt that the entire house was due for redecoration over the summer. They were very nice about it, and offered to let me stay until they needed to get at my room, but that was only a week. Not that I could really stick around for that long when they were going to turn most of the utilities off.

My first thought, the natural one, was to give up on my independence for a while and make for my parents' place in Brittany. It wasn't the perfect solution though – far from it – as not only would I be putting myself under constant pressure to find a job but I'd have completely blown any chance of seeing Julian again. Finding some casual work locally and renting a room would have been a better choice, but there's not much call for a third-class degree in the history of art and burger flipping wasn't going to get me anywhere.

For three days I held off, but it looked like Brittany for me and I was pretty fed up when I came down on what had to be my second to last day in Ipswich. Julian hadn't been in touch either, and I'd begun to wonder if he actually thought of me as no more than a quick shag. It was nearly noon, and the workmen had put the post on the table, two items of obvious junk mail and a large, expensive-looking envelope with a crest. I only glanced at it casually, expecting it to be some sort of fiddle but was surprised to see that it was addressed to me, and by hand.

The letters under the crest read "Aylsham Estates", sending me into a panic as I imagined Vanessa suing me or having me summoned for misusing her bed. I tore open the envelope and my stomach went tight at the formal "Dear Miss Anthony" and the dry tone of the opening line. That stayed the same, but my reaction turned from apprehension to astonishment. It was an offer of a job interview, for the post of assistant manager at Candle Street Hall, and from the secretary of Sir Henry Aylsham Bart. Sir Henry Aylsham could only be Vanessa's husband.

I could only imagine it was Julian's doing, because Vanessa had made her opinion of me extremely clear and I hadn't even met her husband. That suggested Julian had a great deal more influence than had been apparent, enough to persuade a self-satisfied bitch like Vanessa that the girl he'd been bonking in her marital bed was an appropriate candidate for a job. That in turn suggested that Julian wanted me, badly, which set my heart racing as I read over the letter twice more in case anything had escaped me.

Nothing had. It was absolutely straightforward, offering me the interview and providing a phone number and an email in order that I could respond promptly. I did, hoping to get Julian, but finding myself talking to the secretary, who confirmed the offer and asked if I could come over the following afternoon. With that I could no longer hold back. I rang Julian, only to be put straight to voicemail.

Puzzled and frustrated, I set about sorting the last of my things out. Fortunately I'd had good friends in the year below me, rather too good in fact, because they were one of the reasons I'd spent my time partying instead of revising. That did at least mean I could store my stuff, and I spent that night in an almost bare room, thinking of what might happen the next day until I drifted off to a sleep troubled by dreams of Vanessa as Lady Howard, stalking me through the Norfolk lanes with a gigantic, spectral hound at her side.

I woke early, to a day already warm and still. My interview wasn't until mid afternoon, but I was determined not to be late and hoping to speak to Julian first, perhaps rather more. The coach was a lot busier than before, the bus hot and stuffy, so that the journey to Candle Street seemed to last for ever. I was supposed to go to the estate offices, which I'd assumed would be in the Hall but turned out to be in a red brick gatehouse at the beginning of the drive, which I'd passed on my way home before but failed to notice the sign. It was very different to Candle Street Hall itself, with double-glazed windows opening into white-painted rooms and everything seeming very brisk and efficient. I didn't need to be there for an hour, but made the mistake of pausing to read the historical information on the Hall, which was displayed on a huge board beside the drive.

'You're early, Chloe, which I shall take as a sign of efficiency.'

It was Vanessa, speaking from directly behind me and, for the second time, nearly making me jump out of my skin. I babbled something about not liking to be late, but she took no notice, turning on her sharp designer heels and making for the gatehouse. She was still talking, but didn't bother to turn her head.

25

'I suppose I can find the time to interview you now. Follow me.'

I followed, feeling a bit like a puppy, and a badly behaved one at that. We entered the house, passing a room in which a thin man who I took to be the secretary was working at a keyboard, but instead of going into any of what were obviously offices, she clattered up the stairs, still not bothering to look back. The upstairs was a flat – small, comfortable and modern – again very different to the Hall itself. She obviously lived there and I felt a touch of relief that I hadn't after all intruded on her marital bed for sex.

'Sit down.'

She had indicated a straight-backed wooden chair as she spoke. I sat down, feeling rather small, as if I were once again in the headmistress' study and about to be told off for putting a hockey ball through the window of the Senior Common Room; for all that I knew I'd been sat on the plain chair in order to make me conscious of my low status next to Vanessa. She poured herself a drink – gin and tonic – made slowly and carefully with ingredients taken from a small fridge within what looked like an antique sideboard. I didn't get offered anything, and when she sat down it was on the big sofa opposite me, with her long legs crossed and the toe of one shoe pushed out as if she expected me to go down on my knees and kiss the shiny black leather. She took a sip of her drink, then nodded, her dark eyes regarding me thoughtfully, her painted mouth scornful, amused. I felt I ought to say something, but when I began she raised a finger to hush me and I found myself obeying automatically. She was dressed in a suit of fine grey wool – very businesslike, especially for the country, and obviously expensive, adding to my sense of inferiority, because while my interview suit was smart by student standards her own clothes made it look cheap and shabby. Finally she spoke.

'How old are you?'

26

'I'm 23, but I do have experience in conservation ...'

'And you have a degree of sorts, I believe?'

'Yes, in history of art, which I hope would be ...'

'And you've known Julian since you were at college?'

'Well, yes, I ...'

'Can you cook?'

'Yes, quite well. I ...'

'Do you have any strong religious convictions?'

I hesitated, because it seemed an odd question, and one expecting the answer to be yes, otherwise it was hard to see why it would be important. She spoke again before I could find a convincing answer.

'Clearly you have no morals in any event.'

'Mrs Aylsham!'

'Lady Aylsham.'

She went quiet, leaving me blushing and fidgeting, yet not daring to challenge what she'd said. Her eyes were fixed on me again, with that same superior, knowing look, but I finally managed to find my voice.

'Lady Aylsham, look, I know we got off on the wrong foot, but ...'

'Not at all. I think we started very well and I think we shall get on very well, as long as you do as you're told. When can you start?'

I'd meant to respond to her first remark with some comment about fulfilling my duties to the best of my abilities, for all that I wanted to ask exactly what she meant, but her question took me completely by surprise.

'Start?'

'Yes, start work.'

'Er ... as soon as you like, I suppose.'

'Good. Tomorrow, nine o'clock sharp then. You can go.'

I hesitated, astonished by how abrupt it had all been and very sure that wasn't normal for job interviews, despite my lack of experience. She took another sip of her drink then looked up.

'Run along then. You can go and see lover boy if you like.'

'Yes, but ... I mean, thank you, but where will I be staying? How much does the job pay?'

'Graham deals with the money. You can pick a room at the Hall – any of them except the ones open to the public, and that includes the one where I caught you getting your little tail serviced.'

My mouth came wide in outrage and astonishment for her words, but instead of the cutting response I intended I found myself thanking her again and leaving the room, dismissed. I'd got the job, and if the way they ran the estate seemed highly peculiar then at least I would be with Julian, and living in beautiful Candle Street Hall. It was impossible not to feel good about it, so good I wanted to sing.

Graham was the secretary, and he rather grudgingly allowed me to interrupt his work in order to sort out the paperwork necessary to make me officially an employee of the estate. The pay wasn't brilliant, but with accommodation and presumably food thrown in I couldn't really complain. I'd have a lot of free time too, by the look of things, and I knew exactly how I planned to spend that time.

Chapter Four

UNFORTUNATELY JULIAN WAS NOWHERE to be found. I'd been more than eager to tell him the good news, and imagining how we'd celebrate, which left me both disappointed and frustrated, but there was plenty to do. First was my choice of room, and while it was a great pity not to be able to use any of the grand and beautifully furnished main bedrooms, even what had once been the servants' quarters were quite spacious and had wonderful views across the fields to the distant Broads, with windmills and the sails of yachts rising above the hazy green of the reed beds.

The best of the servants' rooms occupied one corner of the building where it turned into itself and overlooked a more or less derelict area of stables and outhouses. Julian had taken it for himself but it was unlocked, allowing me the guilty thrill of looking over his things, although I stopped short of actually rummaging. There was plenty of interest anyway, including some very peculiar books, on haunting, witchcraft, the occult, which I could only suppose gave him background for his job. There was also a skull, from a goat or maybe a sheep, with curly horns and a black candle on top, half burnt down so that the white of the bone was spattered and streaked with wax. I told myself that would also be a prop, along with the bronze pentagram and the dagger of curious oriental design on top of his chest of drawers. The box of coloured children's chalks was a little harder to explain, but only made him seem more mysterious.

I was sure he'd come back and catch me, and be angry, so I soon left. It seemed likely I'd be spending my nights with him, or at least I hoped I would, but I wanted a room of my own anyway. The next best seemed to be the one across the passage, also a corner room but smaller and looking directly across the fields to the fringe of reeds that marked the river. I'd only brought an ordinary bag, but put it down on the chest of drawers to mark my occupation. The bed was bare and I set to work finding pillows, sheets and blankets because they didn't seem to have discovered duvets, all the while hoping Julian would come back.

With my room as habitable as I could make it I spent a while looking around the rest of the house, still waiting for Julian. I was staring out of the window in the room where we'd made love – if that was at all the right expression for the way he'd handled me – when I caught a glimpse of somebody among the trees, some distance from the house. Fairly sure it was him, I went outside, following a path round the house to the old yard and in among the oaks and willows that formed a little wood to the rear.

The rise of land on which the house was built extended quite a way at the back, and only a narrow path led through the woods, although I could tell it had been wide and straight, while the biggest oaks had been planted in neat lines and must once have formed a short but fine avenue. That seemed a little odd, as I was heading for the river, but at the margin of the wood I came across a folly of flint and brick and black iron, which seemed to have been built on the foundations of an earlier bigger structure. It had five sides, with steps leading up from the path between twin pillars and tall arched windows looking out at the woods and across to the distant Broads.

I went in, to find the interior dry and bright with sunlight, the air fresh and clean but tinted with the smell of the woods and something else, faintly organic. There were two stone benches and a dais at the centre, perhaps designed for a panorama of the view but now blank but for a dark stain as if somebody had spilt ink across the stone surface. I wondered if Julian came there to write, and if so whether it would be prose or poetry, and whether he would ever allow me close enough to want to share it.

As I stood there, thoughtfully tracing the outline of the stain with my finger I began to wonder if I hadn't got it all wrong, and if he really wanted me at all. He wasn't there, after all, and it was entirely possible that Vanessa Aylsham simply wanted a cheap and compliant estate worker. I'm very good at working myself into a depression over nothing, and I'd just got to the point at which I was wondering if it wouldn't be best to make straight for the bus stop when I heard the crackle of footsteps on dead leaves. Julian appeared, jumping up the steps, his normally wry smile now broad and welcoming as he took me in his arms.

'There you are! I've been searching for you everywhere. I thought you would be at the estate office?'

'I was early. Vanessa ... Lady Aylsham interviewed me then and there. I got the job!'

'Of course. I asked her to make the offer.'

'And she did, after ...'

He laughed, kissed me on the tip of my nose and carried on. 'We have a ... a funny relationship, Vanessa and I, and she trusts my judgement. After all, it was me who turned this place around.

'Yes. The estate was just about breaking even when I first came here, and now they're doing really well, mainly from TV fees, although the tours bring in a bit. There are practically no overheads, and I've managed to secure grants, but that's all very dull. I'm so glad you took up the job. Come here.'

He'd never let go, and he kissed me again, this time on my lips. I couldn't help but respond, already imagining

31

myself sitting on the dais with my skirt rucked up and my knickers to one side for his cock even as I let my mouth open under his. To my surprise he broke away quite quickly, to run one finger gently across the curve of my chest as he let his breath out in a low sigh.

'Ah, what I wouldn't like to do with you.'

'Do it then, anything you like.'

'Not here.'

'Why not? It's lovely ...'

'I'll explain, but not now.'

He simply picked me up, tipping me back into his arms to carry me outside without any obvious effort at all. I didn't protest, more than happy to be manhandled. Outside, he laid me down in the long warm grass where the woods gave way to a bank. I thought he'd mount me straight away, as rough and urgent as he'd been before, and I opened my arms to him. He just grinned, kneeling over me as he pushed my legs up and open. My skirt had already come up, and he reached under it, to grip my knickers and pull them off down my legs.

I closed my eyes, open to him, expecting his cock, but what I got was his tongue. A little gasp of surprise and pleasure escaped my lips as he began to lick, holding me by my hips with just the very tip of his tongue flicking over my sex. He was teasing, pressing just hard enough to leave me helpless in moments, but not so hard it would make me come. I relaxed, smiling happily as I fumbled open the buttons of my blouse. My bra came up and my breasts were free to the warm summer air, my nipples quickly stiff under my fingers.

Julian saw what I'd done and gave a soft growl, but he didn't stop licking. I arched my back, pushing myself against his face as I caressed my breasts. Nobody had licked me for a long, long time, and it was bliss. So was lying near naked in the long grass, and if I wasn't actually on show to anybody, then I was at least out in the open. I

32

let my imagination run, thinking of how anybody who came out of the woods would see me, with my thighs spread to Julian as he worked his magic on my pussy, my breasts bare in my hands. Inevitably that person became Vanessa, looking down with amusement and a little contempt as I gave in to the pleasure.

This time I didn't try to fight my feelings. Julian had begun to lick harder and his hands had moved lower, cupping my bottom. I'd begun to moan and I couldn't hold back my feelings at all, my head full of rude thoughts as my pleasure rose towards ecstasy and I imagined what Vanessa might do if she caught us. She'd said I had no morals. She'd called me a slut. Maybe she'd take advantage of me, telling Julian to hold me in place as she came to straddle my body, to lift her smart skirt, to squat down over my face, to pull her knickers aside and make me lick her to orgasm just as Julian was licking me.

It was all I could do not to call out her name as I started to come. Julian had pulled my cheeks open, to tickle the tight little hole between, a deliciously dirty detail to add to what he was doing to me with his tongue and one that gave my thoughts a final filthy twist as I went into orgasm. In my mind Vanessa was on my face as before, but facing the other way, her skirt rucked up to expose herself, her knickers pulled down to bare her small firm bottom, her cheeks open to show me the tiny pink hole between, which she was about to make me kiss.

I screamed, wordlessly, which was just as well. My back was arched tight, my thighs locked on Julian's head as he licked, my fingers dug hard into the flesh of my naked breasts and my mind dizzy for what was being done to me and the imagined but glorious, filthy indignity of being made to lick Vanessa Aylsham's bottom. The inevitable embarrassment arrived an instant later and I collapsed back in the grass as Julian finally pulled back. I wanted to tell him, but I didn't dare, and besides, he had

33

other things on his mind.

When we'd made love the first time I'd wanted to suck his cock, and it was just as well. He came around beside me, and he wasn't having any nonsense as he took me by the hair and stuck his erection in my mouth. He was already fully hard, making me gag as he pushed himself deep. I struggled to be a good girl and give him what he so obviously needed, sucking and licking at his shaft. He'd begun to groan in moments, pushing urgently into my mouth as I squeezed at his balls and played with my breasts to show off for him.

It was too much for him almost immediately. He moaned something about how big I was up top and he'd come in my mouth, holding me firmly until I'd swallowed and only then easing himself slowly back. Again I lay back, grinning for what we'd done. He came down beside me, cuddling me into his arms. For a long moment we lay together, my mind hazy with happy thoughts of what we'd done and slightly guilty ones for what I'd been thinking about, which led me to imagine how it would have been if he'd had me in the folly, and why he hadn't wanted to. He had sounded quite serious, making me wonder what was going on.

'Why's the folly place so special?'

'It's a very peculiar folly, and if I tell you it might put you off.'

'Try me.'

'OK, but don't say you weren't warned. You can see we're standing on the foundations of an older building, can't you?

'That was built by the first Baronet, John Aylsham, who also built the new house. He was ... let's say he had some strange beliefs, especially towards the end of his life. Most of all, he wanted to make a bargain with the Devil, but being a practical sort of man nothing would do but a personal meeting and a written agreement. That's why he built the original folly, which was five-sided and is said to have had a silver pentagram laid out on a floor of black marble.'

'What, so he could hold satanic rituals?'

'Yes, more or less, but not the sort of occult stuff you might think. His theory was that the Devil would be drawn to sin, so he held an orgy, with the assistance of a few compliant and well-paid village girls, although I doubt they knew the full story. The Devil failed to turn up, but that that didn't put him off. He tried again, with an even more depraved orgy, and again, and again. Some of the things he did ... well, never mind, but let's just say that if you found out you might not have been so keen on sex in the same place.'

'Oh I don't know. It sounds fun.'

He looked at me, one eyebrow raised, and gave a soft chuckle, which immediately made me suspicious.

'Hang on, this isn't one of your stories for the visitors, is it? You were telling it when you showed us around.'

'Yes, but it's real, and so is everything else I tell them, more or less. It's what I don't tell them that matters, like what causes the odd feeling in the Hall. Anyway, Sir John never did get to meet the Devil, or at least not during one of his orgies. The last was too much for him, he died.'

'What was he doing?'

'Nobody knows for sure, although he was 78 so it's not all that surprising. We can guess though, because all the details of all the others are recorded in his diaries, along with notes on how to make things even more sinful the next time. He never got to write the last one up, being dead, and I don't suppose the other people involved would have been able to write at all, or wanted to admit to what they'd been up to. That was in 1692, not long before the business with Lady Howard, and this part of the country was notorious for witch hunts.'

'So what happened to the original folly?'

'It stayed as it was, more or less, although it may have been bricked up at some point. Nearly 200 years later, in 1884, one of the big oaks fell in a storm and it was damaged. The Baronet at the time, Sir Robert, was superstitious, and his brother, who was the local rector, was keen to cover up what he saw as a stain on the family's good name. They had the place torn down and this structure built on the same spot, and consecrated, so technically it's a chapel.'

As he finished his mouth briefly flickered into a smile, not wry, nor amused, but wicked. I remembered his expulsion.

'I remember another chapel, and what you did ...'

He laughed.

'You're thinking of Amanda, aren't you?'

'Was that her name? Tell me about it, come on.'

Again he laughed, and put his arm around me, leading me away from the folly and back through the woods as he talked.

'You remember what they were like at college? So stuffy, so self righteous – especially Haines.'

'Reverend Haines? He seemed OK?'

'OK? Sure he was, as long as you were one of his flock, or kept quiet. I didn't. I went to him to explain that my beliefs wouldn't allow me to attend chapel any more, but he wasn't having it. He gave me this long lecture too, about my emotional immaturity and how I would come to see the truth with time. I was pretty militant about my atheism at the time, and a cocky 18 year old, so you can imagine how that went down! So I had Amanda over his precious altar.'

'But you got expelled! You were one of the best in the college. Everybody thought you'd get into Cambridge!'

'I didn't mean to get caught! It was three o'clock in the morning, so fuck knows what Haines was doing wandering around. We weren't even noisy, because I'd stuck Amanda's knickers in her mouth to stop her ...'

'Julian!'

'What's the matter?'

'Sticking a girl's knickers in her mouth!'

He shrugged, as if to say he'd had no option, but I was imagining how she must have felt, how utterly humiliated, bent over the altar with her knickers stuffed in her mouth to shut her up as she was fucked from behind. It had been from behind too, because he'd said over, not on, and the picture was clear in my mind as he continued.

'So he caught us, and I suspect the old perv was watching for quite a bit before he stopped us, and enjoying the view. That didn't stop him coming down on us like a tonne of bricks, but I'm sure you remember that bit.'

'I do.'

'So I got kicked out. Amanda got off with a spanking.'

'A spanking? What, from Reverend Haines?!'

He laughed.

'Don't be silly!'

'That's still awful!'

'What, having her bum smacked? Come on, it's hardly the same as being expelled from college. It's been a millstone around my neck ever since. Anyway, what I'd meant to do was leave just enough evidence for Haines to be very sure somebody had desecrated his precious altar, so that he'd guess it was me but couldn't prove anything.'

'What about DNA?'

'I thought about that, but I couldn't see the police getting that worked up over his suspicions, so I took the risk. Anyway, it was that which gave me the idea for the folly. Did you see the stain on the altar?'

'Yes, I wondered about that.'

'It's blood.'

'You sacrificed something?'

'No, I poured off what came out of Vanessa and Henry's Sunday joint one morning.'

'Why?!'

'I'm coming to that. The thing about places like this, and ghost tours, is that nowadays everybody's a cynic, well, too many people anyway. A lot of people know about the low-frequency vibration thing, because you can look it up on the internet. Because of that Candle Street Hall is beginning to lose its mystique. I want to restore that mystique, because when people think it's all just a story they won't pay much and we really only get organised ghost tours and local tourists anyway. But if they think we've got something to hide ...'

He trailed off, leaving me to fill in the gaps, but I'd only been half listening because my head was full of images of the unfortunate Amanda, taken from behind with her knickers in her mouth to shut her up and then spanked for what she'd done. Julian was oblivious, and clearly thought gagging a girl with her panties was a perfectly normal thing to do, and worse, that to be put over somebody's knee and having your bottom smacked was an acceptable punishment, even trivial, even quite funny. The thought was making me shake, but I forced myself to respond to what he was saying.

'So you're setting up a conspiracy theory?'

'Something like that, yes. I let the visitors wander around on their own after the formal tour. Some of them are bound to find the folly, but I'm hoping it's well enough hidden to make them think it's supposed to be out of bounds. They already know about John Aylsham, because I've just told them, so they assume I'm trying to summon the Devil, or something like that. The details don't matter, just as long as the story gets out, and of course I can help it along on the net.'

I couldn't help but laugh.

'And is it working?'

'Not yet, but that's where you come in.'

Chapter Five

I WAS EXHAUSTED BY the end of my first day at Candle Street Hall, not just physically, but mentally too. That morning I'd woken up in my room, an ex-student with no job, nowhere to go and no boyfriend, and by that evening I was assistant manager at Candle Street Hall, with the run of a country house and Julian d'Alveda as my lover. All that would have been more than enough, but my head had been filled with more weird and disturbing thoughts than I could really cope with.

For one thing I was in love with Julian, but that hadn't stopped me from developing one of the annoying and inappropriate little crushes I get from time to time. It's always somebody older and stronger, usually with authority and more often than not a woman. I swear I'm no lesbian, but women like Vanessa Aylsham get to me in a way I don't want but can't do anything about. As if that wasn't bad enough, learning the background to Julian's expulsion had put really dirty ideas into my head, ideas that shouldn't even have been sexy, just the opposite. For years I'd been wondering what had really happened, and I'd always assumed, and hoped, that there would be lots of juicy details, but I'd never guessed it would involve anything so rude, so wrong, as Amanda being gagged with her own panties and then spanked for her punishment. I could feel her humiliation, and I felt deeply sorry for her, but both lewd, grossly objectionable details turned me on and there was nothing I could do about it. The whole thing left me dizzy with guilt and arousal, shock and excitement, to the point at which I just didn't know what to think of myself.

Then there was Julian's conspiracy, but that was just fun and something I could focus on to keep my mind from making what I knew was an inevitable connection between my feelings for Vanessa and what had happened to Amanda. Maybe it's that my imagination is just too vivid, or too kinky, but I knew from long and bitter experience that the next time I came those three unspeakably filthy fantasies would come together in my head, maybe even if I was with Julian, but if I was alone it would be almost impossible to escape. The only way out was his wicked scheme, which also fascinated me and turned me on, but in a much nicer way. When we made love that evening, in my new bed, I came to thoughts of how I'd feel bent over the altar in the folly as he pushed into me from behind.

I threw myself into the scheme, happily agreeing to help him in whatever way he wanted, which turned out to be setting up a fake satanic ritual in the folly. He seemed to know almost exactly what he was doing, in obsessive detail, which meant that my work was going to be very different to the way I'd imagined it before. I'd be helping with the house and to organise the tours, but also dealing with occult stuff – some of it seriously weird. Julian knew that sooner or later his activities would be investigated by people who knew what they were talking about, so there were to be no half measures.

The second day I was there Julian drove me down to Ipswich in the morning to pick up my stuff. I said thank you by taking his cock in my mouth in a lay-by beside the main road, with traffic whizzing past us just yards as I kissed and licked at his erection, and always the chance that another car would pull in and he wouldn't be able to cover up in time. It was a great experience, and just the sort of risky exhibitionism I like, which gave me something to take my mind off Vanessa and Amanda.

On the third day he sent me up to London to buy strange-smelling oils and a special sort of drippy black candle, plus some books from a little gnome of a man who worked out of a basement in the Charing Cross Road. I was travelling for most of the day, and passed the time with thoughts of Julian, what we'd been up to, and what we would hopefully be getting up to in the future. By the time I got back the tourists were already gone and we ate together in the kitchens of Candle Street Hall, sitting by the great stone fireplace and eating spaghetti and meatballs off fine china plates at a huge oak table more than 300 years old. It was so very different from the bustle of London, the old man in his cellar excepted, and by the time we went up to bed I knew I wasn't only in love with Julian, but with the house itself. When I told him the next morning he kissed me and gave me his wry smile, only to grow suddenly serious.

'I feel the same, which is why it's very important to make this work. Vanessa is ... she's OK, but ...'

'She's a bitch.'

'I suppose you could put it like that. Anyway, at the moment I'm the golden boy, but if we fuck up she'd sack us without thinking twice, or maybe ...'

He stopped, clearly thinking better of what he'd been about to say, then carried on.

'Anyway, it's got to work, and she's the one we need to keep happy.'

'What about Sir Henry? I haven't even met him.'

'He leaves everything to her, and he spends most of his time bird-watching and taking photographs. You're bound to meet him some time, and he's a nice guy, but very mild natured – too mild to run a business. He doesn't know what we're up to, by the way, not in any detail. He wouldn't approve.'

'But Vanessa does?'

41

'Vanessa would sell her own grandmother. Let me tell you about her. First of all, this Lady Muck business is put on, or at least, she certainly wasn't born to it. I'm not sure where she comes from, London probably, but if you look around the gatehouse you won't find any photos of their wedding, or of Vanessa with the rest of his family. To them Vanessa is the worst sort of gold-digger, but that's just snobbery, because she's stuck by him and without her drive this place would be broke. He'd never have hired me, that's for sure.'

'But you get on?'

'Yes, fine, but ... it's all a bit weird.'

'How do you mean?'

He paused, not looking at all happy, then shrugged.

'I suppose I'm going to have to tell you this sooner or later. Vanessa ...'

Again he paused, obviously struggling to find the right words, only to shake his head.

'No, I'll tell you later.'

'Julian!'

'It's best, it really is.'

'No, really, you can't do this to me, and anyway, if you're going to tell me you might as well get it over with. You're not having an affair with Vanessa, are you?'

He laughed, clear and open, then spoke again.

'No, but I was. It's over, because I'm with you now.'

Relief flooded through me, but it didn't completely get rid of the awful feeling of jealousy which had been my first reaction. He'd reached out to take my hand and gave it a gentle squeeze, but for all that I was trying to tell myself that what he'd done before didn't matter, inside I knew it did. This was not just some random ex-girlfriend, it was Vanessa Aylsham. If I'd felt resentful and inferior before, now both emotions were ten times stronger and Julian was still talking.

'The trouble is, I don't suppose Vanessa is going to see

things that way. In fact, I know she's not.'

'But she's married, the greedy bitch! And why shouldn't I be with you?'

'Oh she doesn't mind you being with me, she just doesn't see why that should make any difference to what's been going on.'

I was left dumbstruck, completely unable to find words for my outrage at a woman who casually assumed that their affair would carry on and quite plainly didn't care what I felt, but it wasn't my very natural outrage that had sent the blood rushing to my face. That was because I'd come once over a fantasy about the nymphomaniac bitch and had been struggling not to do it again. Julian saw and gave my hand another squeeze.

'Hey, don't worry. I'll tell her, but let me do it in my own time, because if we both get sacked ...'

He gave another shrug, more eloquent than words. I merely nodded, my feelings too confused for me to find an easy answer. For a third time he squeezed my hand.

'I love you.'

I responded the same way, close to tears, and would have gone to him, but at that moment I caught the dull thump of the front door being pushed to. It could only be Vanessa, and she came in a moment later, as immaculate as ever in a tailored skirt suit and shiny black heels, brisk and efficient as she clapped her hands.

'Time for work, you two. Julian, you're driving me into Norwich today. Chloe, you can deal with the punters.'

'But ...'

'Uh, uh, no buts, no excuses. Just do it.'

I nodded dumbly, wishing I could find the courage to give her the answer she deserved, but Julian was less easily put down.

'I don't think that's a very good idea. Chloe hasn't had a chance to learn the routine yet, while I'm sure she'd be more use to you shopping.'

There was a snag, quite apart from my sudden jolt of emotion at the thought of being Vanessa's dogsbody for the day.

'I don't drive.'

Vanessa drew a sigh, as if to suggest that while I was pretty much useless it was no more than she'd expected, then spoke again.

'Then it seems my suggestion is the most sensible one after all, and really, all Chloe needs to do is read your notes. She has all day.'

Julian turned to me.

'Do you mind?'

'Um ... no, I can manage, I suppose.'

'OK then. The notes are in the blue folder above my desk, and don't worry about reading from them if you need to, but I'm sure you'll be fine.'

I'd accepted, and that was that. Only when they'd gone did it even occur to me that we'd had a perfect right to tell Vanessa to postpone her shopping trip, which could hardly be important. Yet it was true that we had to be careful, and the trip would give Julian an excellent opportunity to tell her that their affair was finished. I could only hope that she'd accept his decision, and not try to seduce him on the way home, or threaten him with dismissal, or just laugh in his face and order him to go down on her as a punishment for daring to try and call the shots. Not that Julian would let himself be pushed around so easily, but I had a horrible suspicion that I would, which brought back all my embarrassing feelings with a vengeance.

Fortunately there was work to do, and I threw myself into it, first reading through Julian's notes and then practising my technique in front of the house and in the hall. I knew most of the facts, and the hard part was trying to imitate the cool, slightly mysterious air that came so naturally to Julian. He had it and I didn't, but I could at least dress the part, and the baggy jeans, old top and

44

trainers I'd put on when I thought I'd be working around the estate definitely didn't work. Among my things was the black dress I'd bought for a posh but disastrous date in my second year, as well as a pair of flat black shoes. With my hair loose and perhaps a little more make-up than usual I could manage a vaguely Gothic look, which a visitor with a really flexible imagination might just take for dark and mysterious.

I was completely off guard as I began to strip off, thinking only of how I'd look and whether a black silk rose from the vase in Julian's room would be a nice touch or over the top. It was a hot day, and a second shower seemed a good idea, but as I pushed down my knickers I was struck by a sudden, forceful image of being told to take them off so that they could go in my mouth while I was fucked. At that thought a jolt of shame and pleasure hit me, so strong it was only by running for the shower that I managed to resist, and having to skip naked across the passage made it that much worse. I turned the shower on cold, only to immediately regret my decision both because it was not so much cold as freezing and because that I immediately imagined being made to do it as a punishment, by Vanessa, and before my bottom was smacked in front of Julian.

The image was so strong it left my knees weak and my body trembling as I hurriedly finished in the shower, all the while trying to tell myself that I didn't really want that at all. It was no good though, because while I knew I'd fight like a hell cat if she actually tried to do anything of the sort, and that Julian wouldn't put up with it anyway, it wasn't reality that mattered. After all, no doubt nothing so perverse had ever entered her head. *I* was the one who couldn't help my dirty fantasies, not Vanessa.

Dressed, and once more at least superficially in control, I decided that my best refuge lay in company. On the pretext of finding out how many people were coming that afternoon, I went over to the gatehouse and spoke to

Graham. His dull, matter-of-fact style helped to ground me, but I still didn't trust myself. Once I'd stayed as long as I reasonably could I walked into the village, all the while wondering why I had to be at once so highly sexed and so prone to unsuitable fantasies. I was right in the middle of my month, which went some way to answering the first part of the question, as did the way I felt for Julian, with our relationship still in the first hot flush of excitement and mutual attraction. The second part was less easy to answer.

I had lunch in the village pub, just chicken skewers in satay sauce with a glass of white wine, because I couldn't help but feel a bit self conscious about how my figure would look in comparison with Vanessa. My waist was at least as slender as hers, maybe better, but she was impossibly svelte, making me conscious of the size of my breasts and bottom by comparison. She was a lot taller than me too, although that at least was something I could do nothing about, especially as she seemed to think of three-inch heels as ordinary day wear.

When I'd finished it was still over an hour until I was due to meet the visitors, so I took Julian's notes and a second glass of white wine out into the beer garden. The thought of the tour was beginning to get to me on top of everything else, and I drank a third glass in the hope of steadying my nerves. It worked quite well, and I was feeling really quite confident as I walked over towards the church.

Julian always emerged from the churchyard, ideally stepping out from under the lych gate before anybody noticed him. I tried the same and it worked perfectly, after which the tour was a breeze. Nobody knew I was a stand-in, so they simply assumed I knew what I was talking about, while they were impressed by the atmosphere of Black Dog Lane and infinitely more so by the sense of woe in the Hall itself. By then I had them eating out of my hand and could have got away with anything that wasn't obviously an outright lie. I even joined some of them walking around the grounds afterwards, and headed them off from the path to the folly with a careful judged show of unease, just for practice.

By the time the last of them had left I was feeling well pleased with myself, as well as tired, while the wine had caught up with me and there was no sign of Julian and Vanessa. My eyes would hardly stay open, so I wasn't even worried about my dirty thoughts, and went upstairs intending to sleep for a little before starting dinner. I was gone almost before my head hit the pillow, lying on top of my bed, still in my black dress, with just my shoes kicked off. It seemed like just seconds later when I awoke, but the light had changed, now golden and mellow, but hot where it struck in directly through my window. I lay still, half asleep, enjoying the warmth of the air and the slight buzz of alcohol in my head. It had been a good day, in the end, and I found myself smiling for the state I'd managed to work myself into and the way my mind had managed to bring everything together into one filthy fantasy.

A powerful shiver ran through me at the memory of what I'd been imagining having done to me. I stopped just in time, my legs already coming up and one hand moving by instinct towards my chest. It was not going to happen, I was determined, and yet in my vulnerable state the fantasy was almost irresistible, not despite it being so dirty and humiliating, but *because* it was so dirty and humiliating.

Unfortunately it wasn't just almost irresistible, it was completely irresistible. I couldn't stop the thoughts coming up, and with them the need to come rose up, stronger even than before. Half asleep, drunk and secure in the knowledge that I wasn't going to be disturbed, my efforts to fight my own instincts failed completely. A single, despairing sob and I'd let my knees come up and lifted my bottom off the bed so that I could wriggle my dress up over my hips. Still I was trying to tell myself that I'd keep it

47

clean, even as I peeled my knickers down over my legs.

It was a lie. They went straight into my mouth, leaving me burning with shame for my own behaviour but quite unable to stop myself as the different elements of my fantasy fell into place. First there would be Vanessa, angry with me for putting a stop to her affair with Julian. She'd come up to my room, and after a brief struggle I'd have my knickers removed and jammed into my mouth to shut me up while I had my bottom smacked over her knee. With that thought came another powerful shiver, not far from orgasm, and I'd given in completely.

I rolled face down, lifting my bare bottom as I imagined how it would feel to lie across Vanessa's lap with my knickers off; helpless, humiliated, wriggling about in a pathetic attempt to escape that would only make her laugh. She'd hold me in place, allowing the situation I was in to sink in fully before my spanking began, especially the way I'd look from behind, with the full bare moon of my bottom on show, including the wrinkly pink dimple between my cheeks and my sex peeping out from between my thighs.

My hand went back, to stroke at my bottom, imagining her touching me up before she spanked me, both to turn her on and to humiliate me. Maybe she'd even finger me, or open my cheeks to tickle my bumhole, and before I could stop myself I'd done it, teasing the little sensitive ring until it began to relax. My finger went in, just a little way, and I was sobbing with shame and ecstasy through my mouthful of soggy panties.

Even that wasn't enough. My spare hand went back, to clutch at my sex as I teased my bottom hole. I was soaking, and I knew I had been for most of the day, ready for cock, but ready because I'd been imagining not Julian, but what Vanessa might do to me. Now it was too late to stop myself, but I made one last effort, thinking of myself not over her knee, but his, held helpless in his strong arms as

48

he gave me a playful spanking after I'd admitted how the thought of Amanda getting it made me feel.

I'd found my clitoris, circling the little bud to bring my pleasure up as I thought of how good it would feel, but it wasn't right. It was Vanessa I wanted to spank me, to lift up my dress and take down my knickers, to gag me and smack my bare bottom in front of Julian, with me kicking my legs and wriggling in my hopeless, pathetic struggles. I wanted it hard, so hard it left me sobbing on the floor with my bum as red as my blushing, tear-stained cheeks, and when I was done I wanted to be made to kneel at her feet, to kiss her anus in grovelling, abject apology for daring to steal her lover, and at last, to lick her to ecstasy while I masturbated in a shameless display of my true feelings.

It was just as well I had my knickers in my mouth, or the scream I let out would have had anybody within five miles thinking that another incident had been added to Candle Street Hall's long list of tragedies and scandals. I nearly passed out, it was so strong, and for all the great surge of guilt that swept over me seconds later there was no getting rid of the cynical little voice in the back of my mind, telling me I'd just given myself one of the best orgasms of my life and in record-breaking time.

Chapter Six

I WOULD HAVE LIKED to tell Julian, but I was too embarrassed. He'd spent the day being dragged around Norwich from shop to shop with an ever-increasing load of parcels, something that tends to really piss men off at the best of times, never mind when the girl involved isn't even their lover. And she wasn't, not any more, or so he assured me when they finally got back. Apparently she'd just laughed, but hadn't tried anything with him. I had to be sure, and teased him into letting me suck his cock, then felt bad afterwards because he was as eager as ever despite being footsore and hungry.

The next day was the Sunday, always the busiest day at the Hall, with two coach parties to show around. One was in the late morning, something Julian tried to avoid, but it actually worked rather well, presumably because while there weren't very many heavy lorries the tourist traffic heading for the Broads made up for them. We also had the grounds full of people for most of the day. Several visited the folly, and one even asked Julian if anything happened there, allowing him to make a wonderfully unconvincing denial. That put him in an excellent mood as we relaxed over a cold bottle of wine and a salad thrown together with odds and ends from the fridge.

'You see, it's got to work. We just need something a little more obvious, and some luck. Can you take the tour tomorrow? I want to see if I can get hold of some goat skulls.'

'Goat skulls?'

'Well, maybe sheep skulls, as long as they've got horns. I want five, one for each corner of the pentagram, with a candle on top of each. Afterwards we make a less than perfect effort to clean up and put the skulls up in the eaves of the folly roof so that anyone who has a good look is sure to find them.'

I couldn't help but giggle, both for the image he was conjuring up in my mind and for his sheer enthusiasm. He grinned, but a possible problem had occurred to me.

'What if they call the police?'

'It's not illegal to hold satanic rituals, and anyway I'd just tell them the truth, that it's all a publicity stunt.'

'But that would ruin it.'

'No it wouldn't, because any conspiracy theorist worth his salt would automatically assume I was lying. That's the beauty of the whole thing, because once they've got it into their heads that we're up to something nothing will make them change their minds.'

A sudden, delightful thought occurred to me.

'Do you think they'll try to spy on us?'

'Maybe. I hope so, and something tells me you'd like that?'

I'd immediately gone red, which was all the answer he needed. There was a wicked glint in his eye as he went on.

'If you really want that, maybe we could set it up?'

I made to answer, then stopped, remembering how I'd felt when Vanessa had caught us, and the consequences. All my adult life I'd enjoyed the idea of being caught, or watched – even made to do it in public – but I wasn't at all sure how I'd cope with the reality, or the effect it would have on my imagination. Seeing my indecision, Julian quickly backed off.

'Just a thought, that's all.'

'No, I ... I would quite like it, I think. It's just that when we got caught by Vanessa I felt really bad. I mean, the way she saw me! But ...'

I trailed off, unable to admit the effect she'd had on me, but my cheeks must have been cherry red and there was a knowing quality to Julian's smile.

'Take your time, but if you are up for it don't think twice about asking.'

'Thank you.'

He'd given me the answer I needed, tempting me, but allowing me to make the final decision. It was also the worst possible answer, because it meant I might actually do it. Even as I took another swallow of wine the dirty thoughts had begun to boil up in my head, of men watching from the undergrowth as Julian took me on the altar in the folly, every intimate detail of my penetrated body on show to them, their cocks in their hands as they gave in to the lust I'd inspired.

Later that night, as we made love on the huge four-poster in the master bedroom, drunk and horny with wine and dirty talk, my head was so full of rude thoughts I didn't know which to focus on. Julian was at his best, masculine and confident in his actions but never failing to give plenty of attention to my needs, yet while he was always uppermost in my thoughts as he took me to orgasm, and as I let him take his own pleasure between my breasts, he was never alone. First it was Vanessa, riding my face with my tongue up her bottom and my own cheeks well smacked as Julian licked me to ecstasy, and then a ring of eager, gaping men, erect cocks in their hands as Julian speckled my naked breasts with his come.

Monday's tour was my second and I did it easily, and sober. I knew I wasn't as good as Julian, and probably never would be, but now that I knew all the stories it was really just a question of leading the group from place to place and making sure none of them got lost. Candle Street Hall itself did the rest of the work, and while I'd become used to the strange feeling in the hall and on the staircase, and knew about what it was, it never failed to impress.

Julian had left early on his bizarre mission to collect goat skulls, and he still wasn't back when the last of the tour group had left. I'd done the shopping and the housework in the morning, leaving me at a loose end, while nobody else seemed to be about. It had been hotter than ever, and very still, leaving the air with a baked quality, while even the birds seemed drowsy. I wanted to cool off, and wandered down past the folly and towards the river with vague thoughts of taking a swim.

One glance told me it wasn't really practical, with a thick fringe of reeds and mud making it difficult to get out to the open water, while there was an almost constant procession of pleasure craft moving both up and down river. After the quiet of the grounds it felt odd to suddenly be in the presence of so much humanity, strangely exposed too, a lone figure on the bank. Hoping to find somewhere better, I struck off at an angle, in among the reed beds, where a duckboard path offered at least the opportunity to explore.

The change was immediate, and striking, from the crowded river with its wide horizons to utter solitude with nothing to see but the reeds flanking the path and a strip of cloudless blue sky above. My immediate thought was that it would be nice to go naked, both to feel the air on my bare skin and because it would feel delightful daring to be in the nude with so many people so close. We were still on estate land, which meant I was actually perfectly safe, so it was the work of a moment to kick off my shoes and peel my dress off over my head. I hadn't bothered with a bra, as it looked tacky with the straps showing and the dress was cut to support me, so I was down to my knickers with those few simple motions. Just that felt lovely, but not good enough, not daring enough. Off came my panties, a delicious thrill as I showed my bottom and sex, again as I kicked them away, and once more as I stretched in the sunshine, fully nude.

Even holding my clothes and shoes felt like cheating, so I dropped them and walked on a few paces, with my sense of daring rising sharply with every step. To be naked was lovely, but to be naked and have deliberately robbed myself of the chance to cover up if anybody did catch me was something else again. A little voice inside my head was telling me not to be silly, and not to be rude, while I was ever so slightly scared as well. All that was good, making being in the nude more special and making me want to be naughtier still. To think was to act. I got down on all fours, deliberately posing in a crawling position with my bottom stuck up to show off my pussy and anus from behind, a pose that would leave no doubt at all in the mind of any watcher that I wasn't merely naked because I liked to go without clothes, but in order to flaunt myself.

My nerve broke quite quickly and I scrambled up, giggling as I moved on down the path. The duckboards were warm and smooth, but on some my weight pressed them down far enough to let water bubble up between the slats, wetting my feet. It was enticingly cool, making the prospect of a bit of skinny-dipping immensely appealing, but I seemed to be deep in a wilderness of reeds with no open water at all, which made it all the more surprising when I came to a hut.

It was old, the wooden planks black and rotten in places, and low – so low that I could see right over the roof of decaying thatch to a stretch of open water beyond, just a few feet away but which had been completely invisible. My first thought was that it had simply sunk into the marsh, but as I ducked down to peer inside I realised that it was a boathouse. There was even a boat, of sorts, an old wooden dinghy with just the bow sticking out above the water where it was still tied up with a piece of ancient cord. Walkways at either side would have made it easy to board,

55

and would still allow me to reach the open water.

I went carefully, expecting the planks to give way beneath me at any moment, but they were stronger than they looked and I was soon at the far end, where a water gate hung crooked and open. The water was perfectly clear and maybe four feet deep, the muddy bottom clearly visible, ideal for swimming, while the edge of the little lake I'd found appeared to be solid reeds except for where the boathouse stuck out. Nobody could possibly see me, except from the air or if they climbed one of the trees I could see rising beyond the reeds on two sides of the lake. That seemed very unlikely, and I was smiling to myself as I sat down and swung my legs into the water, happy to be nude outdoors and confident in my privacy.

The water was cool, but far from cold after a day of baking sunshine. I slipped in after just a moment, sighing with pleasure for the feeling on my skin as I submerged. A few strokes and I was out of my depth, my toes touching weeds but not the mud. I began to swim, out towards the centre of the lake, which was no more than a couple of hundred yards across, then let myself float, my arms and legs stretched out, basking in the warm evening sunlight, stark naked without a care in the world.

Not even the situation with Vanessa seemed to matter any more, and certainly not my wild fantasies. So what if I wanted to be spanked and humiliated by another woman? It was all in my head, and nothing to be ashamed of when I hadn't actually done anything. I had, of course – I'd given myself a beautiful orgasm – but now that I'd given in to my feelings once there was no point in being proud. Next time I had an hour alone in the house I would do it again, only slowly this time, teasing myself as I imagined different situations: not just being put over Vanessa's knee in front of Julian, but having it done with an entire tour group watching as my knickers were pulled off and stuck in my mouth, my dress pulled up to bare my bottom, my cheeks

56

smacked until my bum was all rosy, with my legs kicking frantically and my thighs open to show off my pussy and bumhole to the crowd. Or maybe she'd catch me as I was and spank me for going in the nude, on my wet, bare bottom, then make me walk back to the house still stark naked and all red behind.

That was an especially nice thought, particularly as Julian would presumably be back. He'd see, and take a turn to spank me himself, in front of Vanessa, then make me suck him hard and fuck me on the lawn with me on all fours and his hard, lean belly smacking against my hot cheeks. The thought had me wriggling with pleasure, and I was forced to start treading water or risk going under. I wanted to come, but the water had started to feel colder and the sun was well down among the trees to the west of the lake, glinting gold on the water, and on something else, just briefly, but very bright. Peering close, I made out an angular shape among the reeds on the far side of the lake. It took me a moment to realise what it was – a hide for bird-watching, built low among the reeds with a slit at the front, and the brief flash of light could only have come from the lens of a pair of binoculars or a camera. I wasn't quite so alone as I'd imagined.

Just as when I'd been caught by Vanessa, realising I was being spied on was more of a shock than a thrill. It was scary too, because I had no idea who was watching me or whether they'd be content with seeing me naked. I struck out for the shore, swimming fast now, scrambled out of the water and ran back the way I'd come. For one awful moment I thought somebody had stolen my clothes and I was going to have to run back along the river bank in the nude, in full view of every single boat that passed. I was sure I knew where I'd dropped them, and they weren't there, but after an instant of panic I caught sight of something black – my dress – further along the path and hanging among the reeds. My shoes were beside it, neatly arranged on the duckboards, but my panties were missing.

Somebody had been interfering with the clothes, presumably the same man who'd been watching me, and he'd stolen my knickers. I didn't even stop to put my dress on, but ran on along the duckboards, no longer caring how many holidaymakers saw me in the nude just as long as I could be somewhere public, but knowing I was safe did nothing to stop my embarrassment as I scrambled up to the top of the bank to find a long, low motor cruiser directly opposite me. It must have been hired for a stag party, or maybe by a sports club of some sort, because the entire deck was crowded with muscular young men.

For one awful moment we stood staring at each other, they with cans of beer halfway to their lips or with mouths open in frozen conversation, me stark naked with my dress and shoes in my hands, my bare breasts and pussy on show to maybe 20 pairs of interested male eyes. We reacted at the same time, they with whoops of delight and encouragement, me by frantically trying to pull my dress down over my head, realising too late that it was both upside down and inside out, losing my balance and tumbling over backwards, legs wide, to show them even more than they'd been demanding before I rolled back down the bank and out of sight. Their laughter washed over me as I struggled with the dress, my face hot with blushes as I cursed them – the panty thief and men in general.

Nobody was coming along the duckboards, and I waited until the sound of their voices had faded before once more climbing the bank, now sure that all those who'd seen me would have moved further along the river. My face was still red as I hurried back toward the Hall, while my fingers were shaking. Only when I was halfway across the field did I slow down, worried that the panty thief might be lurking in the woods behind the folly, perhaps even watching me as I approached. I stopped, wishing I'd brought my mobile so that I could call Julian.

My heart jumped as somebody stepped out from among the trees, but my fear immediately gave way to relief. It was Vanessa, and I'd never imagined I could be so glad to see her. She'd seen me, and I waved and hurried forward, only to turn again at the sound of a shout from behind me. A man was coming across the field – tall, rangy, his aristocratic face set in a scowl. I walked on, fast, as Vanessa called down to me.

'There you are, Chloe. Have you seen Julian?'

'No, but ...'

'He must be somewhere. Henry, have you seen Julian?'

I glanced back to the tall man.

'Henry?'

She looked at me as if I were a particularly stupid child.

'Yes – Henry. My husband. Surely you've met?'

Chapter Seven

IT WAS HARD TO know what to do. I couldn't even be completely sure that Henry Aylsham was the peeping Tom and panty thief, and I wasn't about to accuse him when he was sure to deny everything. Even if I had been certain I wouldn't have been able to prove it, and Vanessa was sure to take his word over mine. I wasn't prepared to let it go, and told Julian as soon as he got back.

'I went for a swim earlier, in that little lake among the reeds. A man was watching me from a hide. I think it was Sir Henry.'

We were in the old stables at the back, Julian sorting through the large box full of sheep skulls he'd brought back. He didn't even turn around.

'Sounds fun.'

'It wasn't. I was scared. He stole my knickers too.'

'He did? But you knew it was him?'

'No! Not until Vanessa introduced us, anyway. I'm not even sure it was him, but he'd come from that direction and I didn't see anyone else.'

'Then it was him. There's no other way to get to that area, except by boat, and we keep the Watergate on the main channel locked. But don't worry about it. Henry's harmless.'

'I didn't know that!'

'Hey, hey, it's all right.'

He put down the skull he'd been examining and came to take me in his arms, holding me for a long time before kissing my forehead and disengaging. I'd needed the cuddle and it did make me feel better, but he obviously didn't take what had happened entirely seriously as he went on. 'So, why weren't you in your knickers?'

'I was skinny-dipping, and ... and I just wanted to go bare. I didn't think anybody would be about!'

'And Henry was, but he was bound to watch, wasn't he? I mean, what man wouldn't?'

'A gentleman?'

Julian's snort of amusement was all the answer my question needed, and I could see his point but that didn't soothe my feelings.

'But he didn't have to steal my panties! And I was seen by this big group of lads on a boat, and ... and I fell over. It was really embarrassing!'

'I thought you loved that sort of thing?'

'Not like that! I ... I don't know, maybe it would have been OK if I hadn't been scared. What do you think I should do?'

'I don't know, really. I could speak to Vanessa?'

'Maybe, but he'd just deny it and I'd end up looking bad.'

'He'd more likely tell her that it's his land and you shouldn't have gone skinny-dipping if you didn't want him to see you.'

'He was spying on me!'

'I'm just telling you how I think he'd respond.'

'You're probably right. Forget it then. Maybe I'm just being hysterical.'

'No you're not, especially as you didn't know it was him, and OK, so any man who sees you naked is bound to want to watch, but stealing your knickers is pushing it.'

'Yeah, the dirty bastard!'

Julian gave a shrug and I immediately found myself wondering if he thought I was a hypocrite. After all, I'd told him I quite liked the idea of being watched. We went silent for a while, Julian sorting out the best skulls as I tried to get my head around the way I felt. There was no question at all in my mind that peeping Toms and panty thieves were perverts, but if men saw me by accident that seemed OK, at least as long as it was what I wanted. Not that they could be expected to read my mind, which brought me a moment of self-realisation, that if I wanted to show off I wasn't really in a position to criticise anybody who enjoyed the view, accidentally or on purpose and whether or not I found them attractive.

Julian had decided on the five nicest skulls. 'Are you all right? If so, let's go down to the folly.'

I'd been waiting for the moment for days, but I just didn't feel in the mood. On the other hand I didn't want to disappoint Julian, or to have him think I was going to chicken out.

'Maybe a glass of wine first?'

'Good idea. Hold these.'

He passed me two of the skulls, taking the other three himself and admiring the horns on one as we walked across the yard.

'These should do the trick, don't you think?'

'Yes, definitely.'

He gave a wicked chuckle and put the skulls down on the table as we entered the kitchen. I didn't know where he'd got them and I wasn't sure I wanted to. The smooth hard bone felt odd, a bit creepy, but he obviously didn't care in the least, sorting out the black candles and the other things I'd bought in London while I opened a bottle. I really wanted to be in the right mood, and poured us both big glasses, downing half of mine in a gulp before refilling it. He took his more slowly, his expression both thoughtful and amused as he sipped the cool liquid, his eyes only occasionally flicking to my face or chest. I couldn't help but respond.

'Do you like what you see?'

'Very much, as you know.'

I nodded, fully aware of what my chest seemed to do to him, for all that I've always felt a bit heavy and clumsy next to women like Vanessa. He grinned back and took another swallow of wine, then began to pack the bits and pieces into a box. It was going to happen, and I could feel my excitement rising with the buzz of alcohol from the mind. I was safe now, although I now knew I'd never really been in danger, and the thought of being nude outdoors was once more a thrill. Graham would have gone home long ago, and Vanessa had been looking for Julian in order to tell him they were going out to a restaurant for the evening and not to shut the main gates. We were alone. I poured out the rest of the bottle, drank and got to my feet, already a little dizzy after the long hot day with nothing to eat.

'I'm ready.'

Outside it had begun to grow dark, the sun now below the horizon and the colour rapidly draining from the scenery as we walked. Julian had the box and I used a torch to light our way, making the shadows flicker as we moved through the wood and throwing the folly into stark relief against the sky. Only the door showed, and it looked black within, setting my pulse racing as we climbed the stairs.

'Hold the torch. Shine it on the altar.'

I did as I was told, happy to let him lead. He put down the box and began to set out the contents, his strong brown arms moving across the yellow patch of light. I knew he meant to make it look good, but he was obsessive, repeatedly consulting a little red notebook as he worked; first dipping a finger into a pot of purple wax to draw the pentagram with swift, precise motions, setting out the five skulls and carefully placing a candle on each before lighting them, only then copying out a set of symbols, frowning in concentration all the while. He worked in silence and I didn't interrupt, so that it came as a shock when he spoke. So did his words.

'Are you wet?'

My response was an embarrassed nod. I knew I was – badly wet – my body responding to him and what was going to happen to me.

'Good. Strip.'

It was an order, sudden and harsh, his tone adding to my feelings and I let my dress slip from my shoulders and stepped free of my shoes and the puddle of black cloth I'd made around my ankles.

'Let me help you up.'

I climbed onto the altar, now trembling badly and very aware that while the night was utterly black beyond the five arches that opened to the woods and fields, we would be easily visible, my body bathed in golden light, naked, the deep shadows accentuating my heavy breasts and the curve of my waist and hips, my hair a dark halo. Julian watched, approving as I took the position we'd agreed on, flat on my back with my head, arms and legs spread out into the pentagram, each between a pair of skulls. He nodded, his eyes fixed between my legs and I found myself blushing for the intimacy of the show I knew I was giving him.

'Don't move at all.'

He had taken hold of my ankles as he spoke, and lifted my legs, keeping them high and open. I took grip on the far sides of the altar, holding myself in place, my breathing now deep and even for my exposure and in anticipation of what was to come. Again he nodded and his tongue flicked out to moisten his lips. His hands went down, to tug open his zip and pull out his cock, thick and pale in the yellow light, already half stiff. It went straight in my mouth, his hand gripped lightly in my hair as he fed himself in and out, stiffening rapidly to the motion of my lips and tongue.

'Good girl. That's nice ... make me hard, Chloe.'

I didn't need telling, the taste and feel of his cock as it

grew in my mouth making me increasingly eager. Now stiff, he began to masturbate into my mouth, an unspeakably rude thing to do to a woman, but when my hand moved to my tummy I got a sharp response.

'No. Stay still, Chloe.'

I nodded on my mouthful, frustrated but enjoying being under his command. He let go of my hair and began to stroke my breasts, teasing my nipples to erection one by one and kneading gently at my flesh. I began to arch my back for sheer pleasure, but got a finger wagged in my face for my trouble and went back to concentrating on his cock as I struggled to subordinate my pleasure to his. His hand went lower, to cup my pussy, one finger between my lips as he massaged me, something I defy any woman to put up with and not wriggle at least a little. I got my pussy slapped.

'Stay still!'

He'd stepped back, his cock a rigid bar, sticking out from his open fly above his balls. I kept my mouth open, quite willing to be made to carry on sucking, but he moved back between my legs. My thighs were wide and high, and pussy soaked and ready, completely vulnerable to him and he got into position, pressing his cock to my flesh. He went in and a cry of pleasure spilt from my lips as I filled, followed by a moan as he withdrew again.

'Fuck me, Julian, please!'

'Shush.'

I bit my lip, trying to do as I was told, but he'd begun to tease me, using the head of his cock to rub my clit and spread my sex, popping himself inside again and again, until I was shaking my head from side to side in frustrated ecstasy and I could feel the juice running down between my cheeks to wet the warm stone beneath my bottom. When at last he put it right in and began to thrust I was gasping immediately, lost to everything but the pleasure of having him inside me and desperate to come while I was fucked. Again I reached down, only to have my hand slapped.

'Will you stay still, Chloe!'

My response was a pathetic mewling noise, then a squeak of alarm as he took hold of my wrists, pressing me down onto the altar as he began to fuck me in earnest. I felt utterly helpless, trapped by his strength and weight, and by my own ecstasy, unable to fight as I lay there, nude and penetrated, gasping and sobbing as he pumped into me, faster and faster, only to suddenly stop, his cock jammed to the hilt inside me. He'd come, but he held himself deep, then gave a few more hard pushes, all the while keeping me firmly pinned in place.

Never once had he taken his own pleasure without allowing me mine, and this time was no different. When he finally pulled out he went down on me, something a lot of men won't do when they've come. Not Julian. He licked and kissed and teased, all the while with my thighs held in a powerful grip to stop me moving, taking his time before finally bringing me to ecstasy at the tip of his tongue, and for once my whole being was focused on him as he brought me to a long, shuddering climax.

I lay back, panting gently, my back and bottom now uncomfortable on the hard stone, something I hadn't been aware of at all a moment before. Julian lifted me, very gently and with exaggerated care, setting me on the floor and giving me a brief cuddle and a kiss before turning back to the altar. There, on the pale stone, was a perfect impression of the turn of my bottom cheeks and the slit between, marked out in my juices and in his. He gave a happy nod.

'That will make them think.'

We tidied up with great care, making it look as if we'd dismantled the ritual in a hurry but while making a serious attempt to hide what had happened. In practice it was all carefully judged so that anybody making a careful inspection of the altar could work out that a girl had been fucked in a pentagram, while if they chose to search under the eaves of the folly they would find the sheep skulls, the candles and the wax.

I would have been impressed, and not a little frightened, had I stumbled across the folly without knowing the truth, but as it was I felt great. Somebody was going to find it, and it was me who'd been had on the altar, me who'd been the object of adoration for the ritual. The only way it could have been better was if somebody had watched us, and after the events of the afternoon I wasn't sure if I'd be able to cope if that really happened.

The next problem was making sure the right people found the altar without giving ourselves away. That wasn't easy, as while the internet made it simple to find people who would jump at the chance of exposing our satanic practices we couldn't exactly invite them to come to Candle Street Hall. I felt it was best to wait and trust to luck, because a lot of our visitors were interested in the occult and in trying to get at the truth behind phenomena, although so far none of them had managed to figure out what caused the sense of dread in the hall. Julian was more proactive, and keen to impress Vanessa with some concrete results. He was thoughtful as we ate and shared a second bottle, only to suddenly rap the handle of his knife on the table, startling me out of the state of sleepy satisfaction I'd fallen into.

'What we need is a dog.'

'We do?'

'Yes, the biggest, blackest one you can find ... No, on second thoughts that's exactly what we don't want. What we really want are paw prints but no dog. Then again ...'

He trailed off, but I wasn't putting up with him being mysterious, not with me.

'Explain.'

68

'We start the tour in Black Dog Lane, don't we? So imagine you'd just heard the story of Black Shuck and John Aickman, and as you walked up the lane you saw a trail of enormous paw prints.'

'I'd think somebody had been out walking their Great Dane.'

'What if they were really big – as wide as a human foot?'

'I'd think you'd planted them.'

'You're a cynic, Chloe, but you're probably right. Damn, I thought I was on to something.'

'No, it's a good idea, but maybe the prints should be along the path to the folly, on the lawn even – perhaps make it look as if we'd tried to cover them up.'

'That's good. Clever girl, but that might be too long after we'd told them the legend of Black Shuck. OK then, not the prints of a dog, but cloven hooves. After all, John Aylsham was trying to summon the Devil, and there are no cows or anything on the estate. Better still, anybody looking closely would see that the tracks were made by something with two legs, not four, but we'd have to make it look good. You were good at art, weren't you?'

'Fairly, I suppose. I did it at A-level.'

'Then you can make me a pair of hoof boots, and in a week or two the Devil really will be stalking Candle Street Hall.'

Chapter Eight

IT ONLY TOOK JULIAN d'Alveda and me a few days to prepare Candle Street Hall for a visit from the Devil. All the equipment we needed was already there, among the gear needed for the estate, except the hoof-shaped boots that were essential to the plan. Those Julian purchased from an online company dedicated to providing kinky footwear for transvestites, because we needed the right shape but nothing made for women would fit. They were black leather and knee length, with zips to do them up, easy to get on and off. I knocked off the heels and fixed my carefully carved hooves to the soles, with brilliant results.

Not only did Julian leave footprints like those of an impossibly large goat walking on its hind legs, but he looked amazing. He was over six foot anyway, but with the boots on he was nearer seven and had to walk with a long, open stride, more animal than human. Watching him come towards me through the woods in the evening gloom was eerie and, if I hadn't known it was him, I'd have run – and kept running until I was in Norwich, or preferably London. As it was he made me feel small and vulnerable, but in a very sexy way, so much so that I insisted he take me then and there, with me kneeling in one of the windows of the folly with my bottom pushed out at the right height for him to enter me. It wasn't very comfortable, but it felt great, with my head full of images of him stalking me through the woods, catching me and fucking me to leave me pregnant with the Devil's child.

71

I told him what I'd been thinking about afterwards, which had him laughing and grinning, well pleased both with our work and with me. That night I told him more, admitting to my fantasies about being caught by Vanessa, if not the juicy details. To my surprise and delight it turned him on as much as it did me, only without the guilt. I got taken again, this time hard and fast, because I'd got him so turned on he couldn't hold back. I had hoped he'd take his time and be rude with me, but there was still a happy smile on my face as I drifted towards sleep with his arms still around me.

We'd tried to leave some hoof prints, but it hadn't rained in over a week and the ground was too hard to take a good impression. All we had were a few scuff marks among the leaves on the path, too faint to be spotted by accident. We needed a wet night, and the right group of people not too long after, leaving both of us keyed up and expectant as one dry, sunny day followed on the heels of the next.

Everything else was perfect. I'd been drunk and horny when I'd told him about Vanessa, but even then I'd been worried he think I was unfaithful, or a slut. His reaction had surprised and delighted me, making our relationship more open, and he'd taken to talking dirty to me during sex, describing how I looked in whatever rude position he'd put me in and what would be showing to Vanessa if she caught us. Once he went further still, describing what Vanessa would do to me, but it was only to lick her, which gave me a lovely orgasm but fell far short of the filthy details I'd been imagining.

The weekend was busier than any other I'd known, with both Julian and I struggling to cope with two full coachloads of tourists, most of whom were German. They left us exhausted, and once the last of them had gone we fell into what had become a regular evening routine more gratefully than ever, drinking cold white wine at the kitchen table while we prepared dinner together. A second bottle followed the first, leaving me feeling mellow and ready for bed. It was still light, but we went up anyway, sharing the shower and drying off together before tumbling onto Julian's bed. I was face down, and he began to massage my neck with his fingertips, something I could never resist.

He knew I was tired and he took his time, not saying a word as he soothed the muscles of my neck and shoulders, moving lower only when I'd begun to sigh with contentment. Even then he concentrated on my legs and back, bringing my pleasure very slowly higher until, at last, I wanted more than he was giving and had begun to push up my hips. Seeing how excited I was, he gave a soft chuckle.

'Be patient, Chloe.'

As he spoke he slapped my bottom, not hard, but that didn't matter. That single gentle pat brought my fantasy of being spanked back, more urgent than ever, and I was too drunk and too horny not to respond.

'Go on then.'

'Go on what?'

'What you just did. Do it again, if you like.'

He did, no harder than before, then moved back to massaging my back. I gave him an encouraging wiggle but he ignored me and, with that, I gave in to my need.

'Spank me, Julian.'

My words were a whisper, my voice full of embarrassment, which grew sharper as he replied.

'Spank you? What, as if you've been a naughty girl?'

'Yes. Please, Julian, spank me, spank my bottom, just as if I've been a naughty girl.'

He gave a soft chuckle and his hand moved down to touch me where I wanted, and to spank me, stroking and squeezing at my cheeks, giving me a sudden, sharp smack, stroking and squeezing again, smacking again. Now it was hard enough to make my skin tingle, a lovely sensation anyway but so much better for the thoughts in my head, the way he'd called me a naughty girl, and how what he was doing might become a punishment or be done to humiliate me in front of Vanessa, or by Vanessa. Now I could tell him.

'I ... this is what Vanessa should have done to me when she caught us. She should have smacked my bottom for me ... Spanked me, in front of you.'

'I wish she had.'

'So do I, on my bare bottom with my knickers in my mouth.'

'With your knickers in your mouth?'

'Yes, to shut me up, the way you did with Amanda when you had her in the chapel. She got spanked, didn't she?'

'Yes.'

'I suppose they did it to her bare?'

'I'm not sure. Probably.'

My response was a low moan and to lift my bottom.

'Go on, harder Julian – really spank me.'

'You deserve it, that's for sure! Bad girl!'

I'd stuck my bottom right up, meeting the now firm swats of his hand. It stung, a lot, but I didn't mind, more than happy to cope with the hot, sharp pain for the knowledge that I was being spanked, by Julian, and not only was he enjoying my bum but he obviously found my wriggles and gasps both sexy and amusing. That alone would have been enough to come over, but he carried on talking.

'Maybe I should call Vanessa and let her listen to the way you squeal and the sound of the smacks?'

'No!'

'No? I'm sure she'd like to listen to your spanking. She'd probably come over, if I asked.'

'No ... no, Julian, but don't stop, and don't stop talking.'

He laughed and carried on.

'I really think I should. She'd love to watch. Maybe she'd even help – help me to spank your naughty bottom, Chloe, to spank your naughty bottom!'

As he spoke he delivered one hard smack with each of the final words, making me cry out in my pain, which seemed to turn him on even more. He grabbed me by the waist, ignoring my squeak of surprise as he hauled me across his knee, now in proper spanking position with my head hung down and bottom stuck up in the air. Again he set to work, harder still, to set my legs kicking up and down and my hair flying as he spanked me, all the while telling me what a naughty girl I was and threatening to call Vanessa and have her join in. It hurt like anything, taking me completely out of myself, to a place where I could no longer control my body, but when he finally stopped I was instantly begging for more.

'Carry on, please, Julian ... spank me.'

'Oh, don't worry, I haven't finished with you, not by a long way.'

I craned around, wondering what he was doing, just in time to see him pick up the black cotton knickers I'd been wearing under my dress. It was obvious where they were going and, as he balled them up in his fist, I'd began to sob, but my mouth was already open as he pushed them at my face. In they went, my discarded knickers crammed into my mouth to gag me and add to my already burning humiliation as Julian went back to spanking my bum.

Now I was lost, completely, in the nude with my own knickers in my mouth as a gag, my bottom ablaze and every rude detail of my sex and bum on show, and, as he spanked, telling me how he'd like to see it done by another woman. I had to come; there was no choice. Utterly brazen, I cocked my thighs wide over Julian's leg to rub my pussy on the hard muscle of his thigh.

'You dirty little bitch! You're not joking you need to be

spanked. Look at yourself, Chloe!'

I couldn't see, but I could imagine, my body bucking up and down as I masturbated on his leg, my bottom bouncing to the spanks and already cherry red, my cheeks wide to show off my sopping pussy and the tight dimple of my bumhole, all on show, all available for him to do with as he pleased. With that thought I came, utterly uninhibited as I brought myself off on his thigh, and all the while with his hand slapping at my bottom, as hard and as fast as he could.

When I woke up the next morning I felt awful for what I'd done, betraying every other woman on the planet by letting a man beat me – *and* getting off on it and behaving in a way I'd never thought possible to any girl who hadn't been coerced. Yet I had done it, and there was no denying I'd enjoyed it – the pain and humiliation both. What saved me from my ill feelings was Julian, who was not merely happy about my behaviour but delighted, and more loving than he had ever been before. He also realised that I was down, and guessed why, which led to a long explanation about how my reaction came from social pressures that had no real meaning. To him I had enjoyed myself and we had harmed nobody, so it had to be all right. His argument made sense, and I wanted to accept what he was saying, but I was left with a sense of having changed, that by giving in to my darker fantasies I had made myself something of an outcast. After all, it wasn't something I was going to admit to my friends, for all that I'd broadcast the fact that I was going out with Julian to pretty much every single person who knew me. I also had a sore bottom, which I told myself I deserved. Therefore I'd been punished for what I'd done, and that helped to make me feel better, although Julian couldn't understand my logic.

Monday was much more relaxed, with only a moderate-sized group, which Julian took while I did the weekly shop.

That meant taking a bus to the nearest supermarket, over five miles away, and by the time I got back the last of the visitors were leaving. Julian was at the gate, speaking to a very earnest couple who continued to converse together in low voices as they walked away. It was hotter than ever, also close and humid, and I was very glad when Julian kissed me and took hold of the bags of shopping as I reached the gates. As he took the weight he favoured me with his wry grin and a glance directed at the departing couple.

'Do you see those two? The woman says she's a medium. Apparently she could hear Lady Howard's voice as we stood in the hall.'

'Oh yes, and what did Lady Howard have to say?'

'That the house was cursed and we were fools to stay here.'

'Did they find the folly?'

'No. They were too interested in talking to me and explaining about their occult experiences.'

'That's a shame.'

'Yes, they might have been good, although she seemed determined to think of me as an innocent caught up in something I don't understand.'

'Innocent you are not.'

'That's more the attitude I want. Are you feeling better about last night?'

'Yes, thank you. I understand what you were saying, at least, but I can't help feeling a bit dirty.'

'But it was your fantasy, wasn't it?'

'Yes, I suppose so, but that makes me feel dirty too! Anyway, you put the fantasy into my head by telling me Amanda got it after you had her in the chapel.'

'So it's all my fault, and what happened to Amanda too?'

'Yes!'

'Then blame me, the evil Julian d'Alveda, and next time

you get it, you needn't feel bad.'

I couldn't help but laugh, and I couldn't bring myself to tell him there wasn't going to be a next time. Part of me wanted to – the decent, sensible part – but it would have been a lie. He'd put the idea into my head, and I knew from experience that there would be no getting rid of it. Just as I'd once thought it disgusting and unacceptably subservient to suck a man's cock, now I loved it and didn't even feel guilty. Enjoying having my bottom spanked was more subservient by far, but I knew I'd let it happen again. Not that I was likely to have very much choice, if the way Julian was looking at me was anything to go by.

'Not tonight, Julian, please. I'm still sore!'

He just laughed and we carried on down the drive. Indoors we fell straight into our routine, sharing a bottle of wine as we made and ate our dinner. Just to be with him was arousing, and just as I'd expected the last of my bad feelings vanished in anticipation of sex, until I was regretting being sore and would have let him put me over his knee if he'd wanted to. He was more reserved, but he did make me kneel for him once we were upstairs, and for once paid as much attention to my bottom as he did to my breasts. The night before I'd gone down on my knees for him once he'd finished with me, the way I usually did when I'd come first. This time he made me stay in position, kneeling with my bottom lifted and everything on show to him as he finished off over my cheeks. Something had definitely changed and, as I cuddled into him, my head was full of bittersweet thoughts of a future that involved regular spankings, only to have my musings interrupted by the gentle patter of droplets on the window. It had begun to rain.

We did it first thing the next morning. The storm had lasted most of the night, but we woke to bright sunshine and the promise of a day both hot and dry enough to leave the ground baked hard once more. We'd slept naked with the covers off, and I awoke to a slap on my bottom and Julian offering me a black coffee. He was ready to go, his cock swollen with morning blood and his boots already on, a strange sight to wake to when all he needed was fur on his lower limbs rather than leather and he'd have made a very good satyr, and a very horny one. I told him he looked like Mr Tumnus in an effort to get him back for my rude awakening and earned myself another slap on my bottom. My request that he spank me had obviously struck a chord.

It was barely seven o'clock when we went outdoors, Julian still stark naked but for his hoof boots, myself in a bathrobe. He was careful, at first, keeping to the tarmac drive until he was well away from the house, then looping round to the woods and the folly. Starting again from the hard interior of the folly, he made it seem as if he'd come from there first, circled the entire house and then returned to the folly. Only then did a much more wicked idea occur to him.

I'd gone down the folly path, creating the impression of a barefoot, midnight visitor, which we'd intended to reinforce with a set of his own ordinary boot prints. Instead he had me run from the folly as fast as I could, with him stalking behind, his strides longer, the impressions deeper, as if he'd chased me. Then it was down on my knees in the mud at the edge of the wood, as if I'd been caught before I could reach the house and used for sex by the creature I'd summoned.

All that was carefully faked, but there was nothing fake about the way he took me, first squatting over my chest to make me suck his cock until he was fully hard, before putting me back on my knees and taking me from behind. He was really rough about it, his hard belly slapping against my bottom, and punctuated by the occasional smack to my cheeks or climbing onto my back to hold my breasts as he fucked me. I was left breathless and eager by the time he'd finished, pulling out to come over my bottom as he had the night before. He was kind though, burying his face between my cheeks and licking from behind, then rolling me over once more and bringing me to ecstasy under his tongue. No man had ever licked me between my cheeks before, and it was exquisite, but in my head it was me doing the licking and Vanessa on her knees to present her perfect little bottom to my tongue.

By the time Julian had finished with me I was sore and wet with dew, more than ready for a shower and my breakfast. Yet I felt no more than a twinge of guilt for my dirty fantasy as I came. After all, I'd allowed myself to be spanked, so it was hard to feel bad about a mere fantasy, however rude. I was also involved in something deliciously mischievous, and thoroughly enjoying myself. Perhaps it was time to admit that at heart I was the bad girl Julian so obviously wanted?

If our morning excursion had tired me out, then he seemed to have a limitless supply of energy. Telling me to crawl a little way towards the house then get up and walk slowly to the yard, he returned to the folly in a proud, high stepping strut. Once indoors I went to the shower, watching as he returned, now barefoot, then put on his normal boots and returned to the folly, carefully avoiding the hoof tracks on his way but deliberately treading on them when he came back. By the time I had breakfast ready he'd finished, a masterpiece of deception so inventive and elaborate that it deserved to be called art. All we needed was an audience.

Chapter Nine

I WENT BACK TO bed and didn't surface again until nearly noon, waking to find the sun high and brilliant, the day hot and still. Julian was gone, the house empty, and while he'd left a note, it was pretty cryptic, saying that he'd gone to fool the geneticists. While I was attempting to puzzle it out over a cup of coffee Vanessa arrived, gave me some new brochures, told me off for still being in my robe at midday, informed me that we had another coach party that afternoon and returned to the gatehouse. I've always been quite good at accepting criticism, or I like to think so, taking on board what's been said instead of getting resentful, but this time I found being told off really quite exciting, and not so much in spite of it being unfair, but *because* it was unfair.

Inevitably I found myself imagining a rather different visit, when instead of rushing in and out of the house in a matter of minutes she'd given me a good spanking for being so lazy before putting me on my knees to lick her to ecstasy as I contemplated the injustice of my punishment. It was rude – too rude to resist – and accompanied by only a little guilt, even when I'd brought myself to orgasm sitting at the kitchen table and not only imagining the scene but half hoping, half dreading that she'd come back, catch me playing with myself and make the fantasy a reality.

There was still no sign of Julian, and I realised that I was probably going to have to take the coach party alone. That no longer bothered me. If anything it was a challenge, and it was also exciting, because they could hardly fail to see our now dried arrangement of hoof and foot prints. Hopefully some would draw the conclusion that a girl had been chased down, caught and fucked by some diabolic creature, and that that girl was me. Or so I thought.

They didn't even notice; admiring the house, the view, discussing Lady Howard, John Aylsham and the sensation of dread with real interest and enthusiasm, but while standing on the very spot I'd been put on my knees and fucked just a few short hours earlier. I tried my best to lead them without being obvious, but they didn't even manage to find the folly. They were random tourists and had no particular interest in ghosts or the occult, but I was still left astonished at how unobservant they were.

The rest of the week followed much the same pattern, with plenty of visitors but none of them inclined to take the bait. A few seemed to notice the marks we'd left and several discovered the folly as they walked in the grounds, but not one seemed unusually interested, let alone disturbed. Julian thought this was because if anybody noticed evidence of satanic rituals they were hardly likely to alert the Satanists themselves – meaning us – to the discovery, but I wasn't so sure. He would spend a couple of hours each evening surfing the net in an effort to find comments, but while there was quite a lot out there, it was all mundane. Plenty of people were discussing the mysterious sense of dread and the Hall in general, but if anybody had worked out the implication of the prints or the state of the altar they were making an excellent job of keeping it to themselves.

We soothed our growing frustration with plenty of wine and plenty of sex, often taken together in the folly. More and more we would talk as we made love, and I now felt I could tell Julian anything, as no matter how outrageous my fantasies, he seemed to approve. He also spanked me, three times in the week, never as hard as the first, but always in some way guaranteed to really bring out my feelings. On the first occasion it was over the altar, with me bent across the top, my hands gripped to the far side with my black dress rolled up and my knickers pulled down. I could see out across the fields towards the river as he spanked me, with the masts and aerials of boats moving beyond the bank, so that if anybody happened to be standing on the roof of their cabin, or if a particularly large cruiser passed there was a chance that they would see. The second time was less risky, but done in a new and deeply humiliating position. Instead of putting me across his knee or making me bend over something, Julian had me strip, then put me on the kitchen table with my legs held up and my bottom sticking out as if I was having a nappy changed, with every intimate detail of my pussy and bottom on show as I was first spanked and then entered. The third time was more alarming still, and more arousing. Vanessa had arranged a meeting for ten o'clock in the drawing room of the Hall, and with just five minutes to go before she arrived, Julian suddenly hauled me over his knee, whipped up my dress, pulled down my panties and spanked me, ignoring my desperate protests. He had my bare bottom towards the door, and I was in a genuine state, struggling furiously and bright crimson with embarrassment, certain she would walk in at any second. He kept going until he heard the front door open, and I only just managed to cover myself up, which left me flustered and horny for the rest of the morning until we were finally alone and Julian was able to take advantage of the state he had put me in. I still felt guilty about what I was doing, but I'd learnt an important secret: that it was much easier to enjoy it if I didn't have to ask but simply let Julian decide when, where and how it happened.

He kept teasing me, threatening to get Vanessa involved, but I knew he was only doing it because it made me horny. On the Friday I made a bit of a mess of the tour, starting off a few minutes early, so that another five people turned up after I'd set off and ended up going to the gatehouse to find out what was going on. Vanessa was all sweetness and light at the time, telephoning me to wait and bringing them down Black Dog Lane herself, but I knew she'd talked to Julian and I expected to be told off when she came over in the morning.

She was smartly dressed even by her standards, in a lightweight cotton suit, a white blouse, expensive heels and stockings, while she'd put her hair up too, which made her seem severe. I'd been working outdoors, and was still in badly worn jeans and an old top, which left me feeling a complete scruff as I came into the drawing room to find her frowning at a sheath of papers with Julian sitting opposite looking inscrutable. Vanessa didn't waste any time.

'Yesterday, Chloe, you set off early. That caused a great deal of inconvenience.'

'I know. I'm sorry.'

'Sorry isn't good enough. I expect you to do the job you are paid for, properly.'

She was being harder with me than I'd expected, and a sick feeling had begun to rise in my throat as I wondered if she was about to sack me. I wanted to be at Candle Street Hall more than anything else in the world and I was babbling immediately.

'I'm really sorry, Vanessa ... Lady Aylsham, it won't happen again, I promise it won't. Don't fire me, please, I ...'

I stopped, because her expression had changed from stern and humourless to a small smile, cruel and amused.

'I'm not going to sack you, you silly girl. I'm going to spank you.'

Her words hit me like one of the slaps she intended to give me, an appalling shock of outrage and humiliation. Another instant and I'd realised they'd set me up, Vanessa and Julian between them, but the damage was done. Anger, a choking sense of shame and another of self-pity flooded through me, along with relief that I wasn't to be sacked and a weak-kneed arousal I was utterly helpless to prevent even as I turned on Julian.

'You bastard!'

He refused to break role.

'I think it's fair, Chloe.'

Vanessa was quick to agree.

'Entirely fair and, frankly, I expect it will do you a lot of good.'

My words came as weak as my body felt.

'Do me good?'

Julian nodded.

'Yes. You'll enjoy it, but it will still be a punishment, won't it?'

I nodded, because we both knew full well it was true, and that I wanted it from Vanessa almost more than I did from him. Only he shouldn't have told her, and I was on the edge of tears as I stood there fidgeting with my fingers, too proud and angry to give in to my deeper feelings and crawl across Vanessa's lap for the spanking I so badly needed. And they were right. It would undoubtedly do me the world of good. She had no such qualms, reaching up to take me by the wrist and draw me gently down onto the sofa.

'Come on, Chloe, over my knee you go.'

Her grip wasn't even hard, but I went, unable to resist the pressure as I was put into position across her lap, my chest and legs resting on the soft material of the sofa, my hips across her lap to lift my bottom into spanking position. I'd given in, unable to fight save with words as she set about preparing me.

'Lift up a little. I need to undo your jeans.'

'No, Vanessa, not my jeans, please ... oh come on, no ...'

Despite my protests I'd lifted my hips a little more, to

85

allow her to tweak the button of my jeans open and draw down my zip. I felt my waistband go loose, and then the jeans were being tugged down over my bottom to reveal the slightly tattered pair of white panties I'd thrown on that morning for my outside work. Inevitably Vanessa noticed, and commented.

'You really are a little tramp, aren't you, Chloe?'

I shook my head, a pathetic effort at defiance. She'd got my jeans right off my bottom, halfway down my thighs, no doubt to make sure everything showed, and as she spoke again I realised that it was going to.

'I think we'd better have these panties down too, don't you?'

'No!'

She'd taken hold of my knickers, but my plaintive wail of distress only made her laugh and I didn't even have enough fight left in me to try and hold them up as the tiny scrap of cotton was peeled slowly down over my bottom. Like my jeans, she took them down all the way, leaving both garments tangled together around my lower thighs and my bottom bare and ready for spanking. I knew my pussy showed behind as well, and that they could both see, adding a new horror to the sense of shame that was threatening to choke me.

I threw Julian what was supposed to be a withering glance, but obviously came across as nothing more than consternation for the position I was in. His response was to squeeze his crotch.

'You're enjoying this, aren't you, you bastard?'

'Naturally.'

I meant to answer, but my words broke off in a gasp as Vanessa's hand found my bottom – not a smack, but a caress. For the first time in my life another woman was touching my bottom, and there was little or no pretence that it was for my discipline. It was gentle, intimate, her long, delicate fingers stroking my cheeks and squeezing

86

gently to feel the texture of my flesh. I hadn't thought it was possible to feel more ashamed of myself than I already did, but the truth was that lying bare bottom across her lap had been a mere prelude to the new and agonising emotion as I struggled not to enjoy what she was doing, and lost. A soft moan escaped my lips and I'd given myself away completely. At that she stopped, laughed, and laid a single gentle smack across both my cheeks. It was too nice to resist, pure and simple, and she didn't stop, slapping my bottom just hard enough to bring home the full implications of being given a bare-bottom spanking across her knee, but not to hurt. Again a moan escaped my lips, and before I could stop myself I was sticking my bottom up for more. She gave a sudden peel of laughter and the next slap wasn't gentle at all, but delivered with the full strength of her arm. I yelped and bucked in sudden pain, but she caught me around the waist and laid in, slapping hard at my cheeks, yet still laughing and talking as she spanked me.

'You do enjoy it! I wasn't sure. I really wasn't sure. I thought maybe Julian was just trying to get his rocks off by having me spank you, but you really do like it, don't you? Oh, you lovely little tart!'

Her words hurt almost as much as the slaps, and I couldn't hold back my response to either – hot, shame-filled tears bursting from my eyes as my body wriggled and squirmed in her grip, my hair flying and my legs drumming on the sofa, no more dignified than when I'd been across Julian's knee, and even less reserved. I couldn't even stop myself from bucking up and down, and I knew my cheeks were coming apart to show off my anus and give them an even better view of my pussy, which was wet. Julian could see, and he was trying not to laugh at me but massaging his cock through his trousers at the same time, provoking a fresh burst of battered feelings for all that I'd never wanted him inside me so badly as at that instant.

Vanessa was enjoying herself too, watching him as she

spanked me and now pausing occasionally to stroke my bottom. I tried to resist my feelings, but they knew, and when Vanessa finally let go of my waist I made no effort to get up. She wasn't finished with me anyway, but had an additional humiliation planned, her hands moving to the hem of my top. I knew immediately that I was going to have my breasts laid bare, and that once they were out it would remove any last illusion that my spanking was anything other than sexual.

'I've always wanted to get a proper look at these. They're so big! Lift up, Chloe.'

As she spoke she had tugged my top up to the underside of my breasts, and for all my feelings I found myself obeying her. I took my weight on my elbows, leaving my breasts hanging heavy beneath my chest as she first took my top right up under my armpits and then jerked up the cups of my bra, spilling my boobs out, naked. She grabbed one, feeling my size and weight, her fingers rubbing on my already stiff nipple until I'd begun to shiver and moan for her touch.

'Very big, and so soft and heavy. I'm not surprised you get off on her, Julian. She's lovely, and such a slut.'

She went back to spanking me, still fondling my breasts as she slapped at my bottom, alternating the smacks with caresses, and her fingers were getting very, very intimate. I couldn't stop her. I couldn't even bring myself to protest, lost in the pain and pleasure and shame of what was being done to me, so that when she finally went completely beyond the bounds of decency and began to tickle my anus all I could manage was a feeble sob even as I lifted my bottom for her attention. Julian swallowed hard as he saw that Vanessa had a finger between my cheeks, and the next moment he'd pulled his cock out.

Vanessa gave an approving purr and continued with my spanking, watching Julian as he nursed his rapidly growing erection. I was lost, theirs whatever they wanted to do with me, just so long as I wasn't left out. When Julian came over I simply opened my mouth, allowing him to feed his cock in and sucking eagerly as Vanessa continued to spank me and tickle between my cheeks. Never had I done anything so dirty, sucking my boyfriend's cock while another woman smacked my bottom, and I knew that it would only take a few touches before I surrendered myself to the final degradation and came under their attention.

I just couldn't stop them. When Julian sat down so that my head was in his lap I went back to sucking, more eager than ever. He took over with my breasts, leaving Vanessa with both hands free, one to smack my bottom and one to tease my bumhole and, at last, my pussy. I was already lost, sticking my bottom up and wriggling against her hand as she began to masturbate me. Both of them were laughing to see my helpless ecstasy as I squirmed and wiggled, my head bobbing up and down in my desperation for Julian's cock as my bottom cheeks bounced to the slaps of Vanessa's hand and her fingers worked their magic on my cunt.

When I finally came it was almost too much, every dirty detail of what I'd been put through coming together in my head to make for an orgasm so powerful I nearly passed out – and as a final, filthy touch, Julian came in my mouth at the very highest peak of my ecstasy. It lasted longer than I could possibly have imagined as well, wave after wave of pleasure in what seemed an endless series of shuddering peaks in time to the hard, rhythmic spanks and the motion of her fingers. As Julian's cock finally slipped from my mouth I was still there, crying out his name, and hers, begging to be spanked harder and promising I would do anything to thank her for what she'd done.

I meant it too, while I was coming, but when she'd finally stopped masturbating me and my shivers had died away I got my reaction with a vengeance, guilt and self-pity welling up inside me, for all that Julian had taken me in his arms and was stroking my hair and whispering into my ear as he soothed me. Vanessa waited, but not long, maybe just over a minute before she spoke up.

'Come on, no nonsense, Chloe. You've had yours, so it's time you gave me mine. Lick me.'

Julian released me and I turned to find that she'd tugged her skirt up and opened her blouse, leaving her small firm breasts and her sex covered only by a bra and panty set of dove grey silk. Her nipples were stiff, her panties moist at the crotch, while there was a wild look in her eyes. I shared a glance with Julian and he spoke up.

'I'll do it. I don't mind, if you'd rather not, Chloe?'

I shook my head.

'No. I don't want you to.'

I really had no choice, or so I was telling myself. It was either give in to Vanessa, or let Julian do it, and that I couldn't stand. So down I went, full of shame and embarrassment as I got onto my knees between another woman's thighs for the first time in my life, my hot, red bottom stuck out behind, my bare breasts lolling forward. Vanessa gave a complacent nod, as if she'd known all along that I'd give in, then pulled her panties aside. She was shaved, her pussy smooth and neat, scented with something expensive that didn't come close to masking the aroma of excited woman. I swallowed, leaned close and I was doing it, my tongue lapping at another woman's sex, a woman who'd just spanked me and brought me to orgasm under her fingers.

Julian was watching too, denying me even the modesty of having my first lesbian experience in private. He'd watched me spanked and now he was watching me lick, and before I really knew it my bad feelings had changed to good, my shame now a pleasure. My hand went back and I was playing with myself as I licked, deliberately masturbating for the pleasure of being made to bring Vanessa to orgasm, and as my feelings rose once more my inhibitions fled. I rose up on my knees, cuddling her to kiss and lick at her nipples, and her mouth.

She was a little taken aback, but responded, letting her lips open under mine until we were kissing openly, our tongues entwined as we explored each other's breasts and pussies. I'd have finished her off like that, gladly, but she knew what she wanted and quickly pushed me back down. Now there was no need for pretence. I'd shown her what I was and, by kissing her, admitted my own feelings to myself. I pulled off her panties and got to work, licking busily at her clitoris with my head trapped between her stocking-clad legs and my hand between my own thighs, my bottom stuck out to show off my smacked cheeks.

Soon she'd begun to gasp and her hands had gone to her chest and my hair, holding me firmly in place as I licked. Knowing she was about to come I put everything into her pleasure, telling myself it was only right when she'd handled me so well, taking no nonsense about having my bottom smacked, or having it done bare, or letting her strip me and touch me up, or licking her afterwards. As her thighs tightened around my head that thought was uppermost – that she'd taken me to somewhere I'd never been and then made me say thank you by applying my tongue to her pussy. It was only right, a thank you for the spanking she'd given me, for realising that my place was over her knee or kneeling at her feet, but for my ecstasy to be perfect I had to submit myself to one final humiliation.

Vanessa had come, and I was once again busy with my own sex, close to a second orgasm. She realised and didn't try to stop me, merely passing some casual remark to Julian about what a slut I was. He was watching, fascinated, and I was determined that he'd see what I was about to do, my tongue poking out, to trace a slow line down Vanessa's sex lips as I picked up the pace rubbing my own pussy, to lap up the juice running from her open vagina, and lower, to tease the smooth bar of hard flesh below her sex, and at last to touch the tight, wrinkled star of her anus, first with my tongue, and then with my lips, my second orgasm exploding in my head as I deliberately, lovingly, kissed Vanessa Aylsham's bumhole.

Chapter Ten

I KNEW I OUGHT to be furious with Julian, for bringing somebody else into our relationship, for scheming to have me treated in such a grossly undignified way, not even bothering to consult me before I was spanked in front of him and then made to lick Vanessa out. It was impossible. I got my full share of guilt and doubts afterwards, but I only wanted to hold him for comfort. He might have taken matters out of my hands in a way that most people would find utterly unacceptable, but I knew I would never have agreed to it and he had not only led me to a wonderful experience but finally made me realise what for years had been nothing more than a very dirty, very secret fantasy. Without him it would probably have stayed that way.

There was no row, no spat of accusations. I simply went for a long walk on my own, along the river bank and the lonely paths among the reed beds, allowing myself to slowly come to terms with what I'd done and accept that the pleasure far outweighed any moral issues, at least so long as my behaviour remained a secret between Julian, Vanessa and myself. That seemed likely, at least to judge by the conversation we'd had afterwards. Henry Aylsham, it seemed, had some rather unusual tastes, and while they didn't go into details, it was plain that while Vanessa satisfied him he was quite unable to satisfy her. Julian had been doing that since a few days after his arrival, apparently with Henry's full knowledge and even approval, but, when I'd come onto the scene, the arrangement had no longer worked. Vanessa had actually been very reasonable, agreeing that Julian should be faithful to me if that was what I wanted, but openly stating that she wanted to share me and had done since the moment she caught us at it. Not that she'd planned to spank me, a rude detail sprung entirely from my own dirty mind, but she had wanted to take charge, and mostly, especially, to have me on my knees while I licked her. Smacking my bottom had been a bonus which she'd enjoyed, as she had the unexpected kiss on her bumhole. For her, that was what sealed it, proving that I was everything she'd hoped I'd be and rather more.

The next few days passed in a haze, with my work a pleasant routine, the Hall a beautiful stage and my life focused on sex in a way it had never been before. With previous boyfriends there had always been that period of delirious bonking, when you just can't get enough of each other, but this was different. Julian made me feel more sexual in myself, more aware of my body, and more attractive. He focused on me both as Chloe and as a sexual being, obsessive over my legs and breasts and bottom and pussy. I'd always been taught to think of men like that as thoroughly dirty, and he was, but as I'd been discovering very rapidly, so was I.

In fact it went beyond dirty, because not only was I doing things which would have had most of my friends talking about psychiatrists, but they had a very definite occult edge. The way Julian handled me was wonderful, but when it was in the folly, with my body laid out at the centre of the pentagram, the candles burning all around me on their skulls and my breasts and belly marked with wax, it was exquisite. I couldn't get enough, and for all my lack of belief in the symbols and rituals we were using, they gave sex an exciting, illicit edge. Julian felt the same, enjoying what we did for the sense of mischief it brought almost as much as he did for the pleasure he took in me.

Both of us were keen to be more inventive. I'd taken to

going nude in the evenings, and in having occult symbols inscribed on my body in wax when we made love in the folly. Julian had taken to his boots, and had me sew sheep skins onto them in such a way that his long, powerful legs were encased in shaggy wool from his upper thighs to his ankles. The effect was magnificent, and as he stood there in the yard outside the kitchen, just visible at the edge of the light with the evening sky behind him; it was all too easy to imagine that some strange creature had come for me. He was naked but for the boots, his cock stirring as he watched me, his wonderful dark eyes drinking in the contours of my body, so that I felt naked before him although, for once, I'd kept my clothes on to do the sewing.

I ran on impulse, out into the yard, dodging past him to flee across the back lawn. He followed instantly, chasing me through the twilight, across the lawn and into the woods. I hadn't realised just how dark it would be and slowed abruptly, laughing as I picked my way down the path, knowing full well he was going to catch me, and what would happen. The trees closed in, the crunch of his hooves on the leaves came behind me and a thrill of fear hit me, half real, half playful. I tried to go faster, stumbled, went down, and the next moment he was on me, his big hands gripping my hips to lift me into a kneeling position.

He just fucked me, my dress turned up, my knickers pulled down, his cock rubbed to erection between the cheeks of my bottom, then inserted. I could barely see, only dim shapes around me, but all the while I could hear his breathing, deep and urgent, and feel him, his hands and cock, all human, all masculine, but also the wool that encased his thighs, soft, ticklish fur touching the backs of my legs and my bottom, first gently as he got himself ready in my bottom slit, then pressed firmly to my flesh as if I were being fucked by the Devil himself, up to his balls in my pussy.

***

It had been a great experience, but only one in a long series, and nothing like as strong as being spanked by Vanessa, or my first time on the altar. Julian seemed to take particular pleasure in it though, and I got it again the following evening, on the moonlit lawn in front of the house with the sky open all around us as I was humped from behind with him on my back, just as if he'd been a real goat. The next morning Vanessa came round and greeted me with a firm smack to the seat of my jeans. It was like an electric shock, going straight to my head and straight to my sex, and had Graham not arrived a few minutes later I would have undoubtedly ended up back over her knee.

As it was I was left on a high all day, thinking rude thoughts of spanking and pussy licking, so that I did the tour in a bit of a trance, not really paying attention to individuals in the group. No sooner had they gone had I stripped off, to spend the evening nude, although to my frustration Vanessa and Henry had gone out together. I got chased again though, caught and fucked on the front lawn for the second night in a row.

The next day was quiet for me, with Vanessa and Julian in Norwich and only eight people on the tour. Later that evening when Julian called me upstairs, just as I was about to start dinner, my automatic assumption was that he was after sex. He wasn't, but was sitting at his computer, fully dressed, staring in rapture at the screen.

'Look.'

I came behind him, to peer over his shoulder, my mouth slowly opening at the image on the monitor. It was a very bad photo, blurred with camera shake and a long exposure, but there was no mistaking the shape of the Hall as seen from the trees on the bank, nor that a couple were having sex on the lawn, she pale and naked with her full breasts lolling down and her mouth wide in ecstasy, he apparently half human and half goat, his muscular buttocks showing bare above thick white fur.

'That's us!'

It was, undoubtedly, posted on somebody's blog with only the tantalising heading that more would be revealed. Julian nodded his agreement and, for a long period, we stayed staring at the screen, the full implications of the picture slowly sinking in. We'd been watched, and photographed, by somebody hidden among the trees. Finally Julian spoke up.

'Last night, do you think, or the night before?'

'I don't know. It could have been either. He was so close though!'

The photographer had been just yards away, peering from the bushes with their camera, peering at us, at me, naked on my hands and knees as I was fucked. It was an alarming thought, frightening but exciting too, and made me wonder how many other times in my life I'd been seen or photographed in the nude or in some other sexually provocative way without ever knowing. Julian was more practical.

'So he was in the bushes at what, between 10 and 11 o'clock? He wasn't there by chance, so he must have been spying on us, which means he expected to see something. Does that make sense?'

'Yes, and either he's got more photos or he's coming back.'

'Both, probably, but I think this was shot with a phone cam, and not even a very good one. Maybe he was with the tour in the afternoon, found the prints or the folly and decided to hang around to see what was going on?'

'Maybe. How did you find it, anyway?'

'The picture is called Candle Street Hall. Hang on.'

He called up the name of the image and began to search, quickly returning to the blog.

'Yes. It's a phone cam image. Come on, there must be some way of working out which night that was.'

'I don't know. I was distracted.'

'Me too, but there must be something. I'm sure we were further away from the trees the first time.'

'Maybe, but even if it was the second time there were nearly 20 visitors that afternoon and we don't even know for sure if he was one of them.'

'That's true. Let's see what else is on his blog.'

There was very little. We couldn't even be certain the photographer was male, although we had both automatically assumed he was. The blog writer called himself The Inquisitor and catching us was what had made him set up the blog. Aside from a lurid background apparently pinched from Hieronymus Bosch's *The Delights of Hell*, that was it. Julian finally gave up, turning me a wicked grin as he sat back in his chair.

'One thing's for sure. He'll be back.'

I glanced towards the window. It was still light, the trees touched with the first golden glow of evening, a scene both tranquil and beautiful but which now held a hidden and exciting menace.

'He could be out there now.'

'Maybe. Shall we give him a show?'

His wicked grin had grown broader still and he plainly thought nothing of going out for sex in the knowledge that we would probably be watched, and photographed. I wasn't so sure, excited but also scared and embarrassed, with a lump in my throat so big I found myself unable to speak for a moment. Yet we had already been watched and Julian was big, and strong, not at all the sort of person a peeping Tom was likely to challenge, although I was definitely not going out on my own. A new thought struck me.

'There were only nine people this afternoon. If he is around, he might well have been one of them.'

'That's true. Do you remember them at all?'

'Not really, no. They were just visitors, one family, two

98

couples and three guys together. He'd be on his own, wouldn't he?'

'Probably, not necessarily. But remember, we don't really need to identify him, and we definitely don't want to catch him or scare him off. We want him to post, and that means giving him something interesting to see.'

'Maybe we could let him follow us to the folly?'

'That would be a good start.'

He didn't elaborate, but the implication of his words was that we would go further. I wasn't sure if I could, at least not unless he simply ignored my qualms, just as he had when he got Vanessa to spank me.

'It's not easy for me.'

'I know, but you'll be OK.'

He kissed me and took my hand, to lead me downstairs. I kept my dress on, and even going about my normal routine in the kitchen there was a prickling sensation at the back of my neck. It obviously made sense to act normally, and yet I was struggling not to peer out at the garden and woods, now bathed in rich golden light with long shadows making shapes on the lawn and among the trees, every one of them a lurking voyeur to my imagination. Julian, as always, took everything far more easily, excited but not in the least scared.

I poured wine, my hand trembling as I filled the glasses, and I very nearly dropped them when I caught a movement outside the window from the corner of my eye. It was only a rabbit, come out to feed on the lush grass at the edge of the lawn. I told myself that if the rabbits were out then the watcher probably wasn't there, a thought that brought relief but also disappointment. It was also a thought I wasn't going to share with Julian, because for all my fears I didn't want to do anything to put him off.

We ate and drank, talking quietly and listening all the while with the door to the yard wide open so that if a rabbit thumped or a bird called out alarm we would hear. There was nothing – only the usual evening sounds – and my confidence gradually increased with the wine we were drinking and Julian's own certainty in his ability to cope with any problems. By the time it was dark I was ready for mischief, just so long as he was by my side, and it was me who finally lost patience with waiting.

'Shall we go then?'

'Yes, but I've been thinking. We don't actually know what he saw, do we? It's possible he saw us from further away – Black Dog Lane even – and came to investigate. He may even think what he saw was for real.'

'Maybe. I suppose so.'

'I hope so, and if so I don't intend to do anything to change his mind. I want him to think I appear in the folly, so I need to get there with my boots. Go out the back and walk around to the front lawn, naked, or in just your panties, if you prefer. If he is watching then that's sure to distract him.'

'You want me to go out alone?'

'Of course. Don't worry. I'll be nearby, and you'll never be far from the house.'

I swallowed hard, considering the route he wanted me to take, out through the yard, around the northern end of the house and across the front lawn, naked or near naked. The moon was up, so strong that even with the kitchen light on we could make out the trees beyond the yard. I'd be clearly visible to anybody watching from the trees, and if I'd also be able to see anybody who came at me, that was very little consolation.

'Couldn't I just stand at the front door or something? I don't mind being naked, but we don't know who this guy is. He might be dangerous.'

'Not when he knows I might be about, especially not if he thinks I'm the Devil.'

'If he thinks you're the Devil then he's got a hell of a lot of guts just coming here.'

100

'That's true, but anyway, there's no point in you standing at the front door if he's watching the back.'

'Won't he know we're in the kitchen anyway and guess it's you?'

'Maybe, in which case he'll just find our behaviour puzzling, which is always a good thing. Or maybe not. Maybe he's not there at all.'

I responded with a glum nod, keen to help but not at all sure about what he was asking me to do. He poured the last of the wine into my glass and sat back, silent. I took a gulp, and another, wishing I was braver, both personally and as an exhibitionist. Julian waited, patient but obviously intent on making me do as he wanted, and it was that calm certainty of purpose that finally persuaded me.

'OK, I'll go, but if I call out come quickly.'

'I'll be there before you know it. Nude or panties?'

'Nude.'

It was what he wanted, I could tell from his voice. He was watching as I stood up and peeled my dress up over my head, kicked off my shoes and pushed down my panties to stand naked in front of him, feeling more than a little like a lamb sent to the slaughter. I cupped my breasts to show off to him and in an effort to feel good about going bare outdoors, but I was trembling badly as I walked to the door.

Outside the night was warm and still. The air still smelt baked from the heat of the day and the leaves of the moonlit trees were barely stirring. I could hear the road in the distance, loud now that everything else was quiet, and a lone engine somewhere off beyond the village. Nothing moved at all. I glanced back to Julian.

'Go on then, and come back through the house, then walk down to the folly. Set up the pentagram, chant, or play with yourself or something and I'll appear as if by magic.'

'OK.'

I stepped out into the night, driven by his enthusiasm and my need to please him. With every step I expected a figure to detach itself from the shadows or the flash of a camera to explode in my face. Nothing happened, but my fears grew stronger as I moved away from the house, out onto the lawns, only to lose my nerve and dash for the front door, running as fast as I could, barefoot over the grass and absolutely convinced I could hear heavy male footsteps pounding behind me.

There was nothing, the lawn empty as I looked back from the shelter of the front door. My heart was pounding and the adrenaline was singing in my head, my shaking worse than ever as I closed and barred the door. Only then did it occur to me that the man might have watched Julian leave and now be waiting for me in the kitchen, the sort of thing that's always happening in horror films. To one side was an ancient stand full of walking sticks and umbrellas. I selected the heaviest stick, a massive blackthorn root more like an Irish shillelagh than a gentleman's cane. Holding it at my shoulder I made a cautious return to our quarters, only to find the kitchen deserted and the door still open to the night.

Feeling slightly foolish, I was grinning to myself as I peered outside once more, and wondering how I'd look, stark naked with the massive stick in my hand, but I kept a firm grip on it as I started for the folly. Walking the path through the trees was worse than being on the lawn, with the ground barely visible and the branches and leaves creating a multitude of confusing shadows. The slightest sound and I'd have run, but I reached the folly unmolested and my soft whisper was answered by Julian where he'd hidden himself beneath one of the stone benches.

Now more confident, because if anybody did come they were the ones who would get a shock, I began to set up the altar in what had become a familiar routine. My thumb was the perfect implement to draw out the pentagram, the outline of which was now stained into the stone, and also to paint the sigils onto my breasts and belly. With that done I went to fetch the sheep skulls and chanced to glance out over the field towards the river, where a dark shape was walking towards me, unnaturally tall, a ragged coat flapping around his ankles, or possibly its ankles, because no human had such an angular, bony head.

I was screaming for Julian and snatching for the blackthorn stick and turning to run all at the same time, my head full of terrifying visions of some grotesque nightmare we'd managed to summon up from hell itself, only to stop as the thing spoke.

'Who's that? Are you all right in there?'

Julian was still uncurling himself from under the bench as I snatched my hands over my breasts and pussy, my fear shifting to acute embarrassment as Henry Aylsham stepped closer. Now I could make out the rucksack on his back and the tripod fixed across it, making me feel intensely foolish as I struggled to find an excuse for what we were doing in his folly at the dead of night, me naked and Julian done up as the Devil. Julian spoke first, and his response astonished me.

'Oh it's you. You scared Chloe. Go to Vanessa, now.'

I expected a furious response, and probably the sack, but Henry merely muttered an apology and moved on past the folly. He'd presumably been out bird watching until sunset, or possibly girl watching, but even then he had every right to be on his own land. Yet Julian had spoken to him as if their roles were reversed. The moment Henry was out of earshot I couldn't help but ask.

'Thanks, but isn't he going to sack you or something?'

Julian laughed.

'No, not Henry. Are you OK now?'

'Yes, just about. He gave me a shock, that's all. There's this book I read, *Banquet for the Damned*, and there's this horrible thing like a giant dog skeleton dressed in rags. He looked just like that coming across the fields.'

'Don't fuss, darling. Nothing like that exists.'

'I know, but ...'

'Hush.'

He hugged me close and kissed the top of my head. I was trembling badly, my body prickled with sweat, but I was a lot calmer and a new thought occurred to me.

'Do you suppose Henry could have taken that photo?'

'Henry? No, definitely not.'

'How can you be sure?'

'That wouldn't be his style at all. Anyway, he knows.'

'He knows? About what we're doing?'

'Of course. It's his estate, after all, and it's probably about time I explained how things work around here ...'

Chapter Eleven

HE DIDN'T, NOT THEN and there, but led me back to the house and a very welcome bed. The next morning he went to talk to Vanessa and came back with a wicked grin on his face, refusing to tell me what was going on. I wondered if I was due for another spanking, and although I couldn't see why, I was sure they'd find an excuse. Not wanting to repeat the embarrassment of being caught in tattered old knickers I dressed carefully, in matching underwear and a smart dress, but as I stood doing my make-up in the bathroom mirror and thinking how easy it would be to strip me Julian called out from his room.

'He was there, look!'

I rushed in, lipstick in hand, to find Julian looking at the same blog as before, the Hieronymus Bosch wallpaper instantly recognisable, only instead of the photograph there was a paragraph of text. Julian began to read it out.

'"This is getting well weird! I went back to Candle Street Hall last night, not with the phone but with my D90, meaning to get some serious shots. The girl was there, naked like before, but she was too far away when I saw her. She walked into the woods where the old temple is so I started walking round. With the tripod I should've been able to get something, maybe, but before I even got close there was this scream. It scared the shit out of me, believe me, and I saw other people, at least three of them, the man who runs the ghost tours and a skinny guy with a load of equipment. What happened? Maybe something went wrong

105

and she got scared, but I aim to go back and find out.'''

Julian and I shared a glance.

'He was watching us, all the time!'

'Not all the time, unfortunately. He seems to know who you and I are though, but not Henry, which must mean he's been on a tour.'

'And he's coming back.'

'Yes, tonight with any luck, because that will give him a chance to investigate thoroughly. We'll be over at the gatehouse.'

'We will?'

'Yes.'

'You're going to spank me, aren't you, in front of Henry?!'

'No.'

'Oh. What then, by Vanessa again?'

'No.'

'So what is happening? Tell me, Julian.'

'You'll see.'

He went back to studying the screen, and didn't respond at all when I prodded his shoulder in vexation for being so mysterious. As before, the Inquisitor hadn't left any real clues, but it seemed likely that he'd either come across the fields from Black Dog Lane or along the river bank. In either case it was easy to get onto the estate, but the marshes downriver were pretty much impassable, while we couldn't really see him simply strolling up the drive. He'd definitely been on the river bank when he'd heard me scream, or we'd have seen him, and Henry had come back through the marshes. Otherwise his identity and movements remained a mystery, but I agreed with Julian that the best thing to do was lock the house up securely and give him a free run of the grounds.

We left the folly more or less as it was, with the pentagram in place and the pot of wax still out, but we added a couple of skulls, all as if we'd abandoned it in a

106

hurry. That put Julian in a mischievous mood, and he added another set of hoof prints, some among the leaves, which barely showed, but one track leading out across the field before turning back, as if he, or it, had started for the river bank where the Inquisitor had presumably been lurking.

There was a big group coming that afternoon, and Julian and I shared the tour. Beforehand the faces of visitors had tended to blur into one, especially when I had my mind on other things, but now I was intent on every face, hoping to search out our mysterious watcher. If he was among my group he wasn't making himself obvious, and while there were four single men, they were together and it was hard to see anyone of them as the Inquisitor. Julian had no better luck.

'Not in mine. How about yours?'

'I don't think so, but I don't really know what to look for.'

'It's hard to say, but after last night you'd think his attitude towards us would stand out. Maybe he came before and doesn't want to give himself away.'

'There's that.'

'Anyway, if you're ready, Graham's gone home so it's time we went over to the gatehouse.'

He took my hand and I allowed myself to be led down the drive with my sense of anticipation rising fast, along with my apprehension. Even though Vanessa had spanked me before and there was no denying that I'd enjoyed every moment, the emotion that went with it was close to overwhelming. Without Julian I'd probably have turned back, but as always he made it far easier to give in. By the time we reached the gatehouse I was shaking again, my head full of thoughts of what was to happen; the moment my panties would come down, whether she'd put them in my mouth again, how painful the smacks would be, and being put on my knees to her when my punishment was over. Julian had no such qualms, leading me in at the door and up the stairs to Vanessa and Henry's living room, where both of them were waiting for us. My stomach went tight at the thought of being spanked in front of Henry, one more witness to my humiliation and a male one at that. Yet that didn't seem to fit in with the way he was dressed, which was startling to say the least.

When I'd seen him before he'd been in baggy, threadbare tweeds, completely unremarkable. Now he was in what appeared to be a maid's uniform, in black nylon with white lace at the neck and a frilly underskirt, also stockings and high heels, while his hands were folded in his lap and his eyes downcast in a hangdog expression. Vanessa was no less striking, in a sheaf of skin-tight scarlet leather, and knee-length, high-heeled boots of the same brilliant colour. She was also holding a long riding whip with a particularly vicious-looking leather sting at the business end. I immediately imagined how painful it would be if applied to my bottom, but she was smiling at me, as wicked as could be, but more friendly than cruel as she spoke up.

'Hello, Julian, and little Chloe. She's going to watch, worm.'

The final word was addressed to Henry, who responded with a shame-filled mumble.

'Yes, mistress.'

Vanessa went on.

'Make yourselves comfortable. Worm, why aren't you getting them drinks?'

'Sorry, mistress.'

Henry hurried to obey, while I hastily closed my mouth and tried to look as if what was going on was familiar. It wasn't – far from it – but I seemed to fit in as a witness to Henry's humiliation and possibly a beating, which filled me with both relief and disappointment but no real excitement. Vanessa carried on as Henry mixed gin and

108

tonic.

'I do hope you can cope with this, Chloe, but Julian assured me you'd be OK and you do like your own bottom smacked, after all, don't you? You ought to see him punished anyway, don't you think, for spying on you at the lake, and for scaring you last night?'

'That ... that wasn't really his fault, and ...'

'Nonsense. It's always his fault. Isn't it, worm?'

'Yes, mistress.'

'And are you going to say sorry to poor Chloe?'

'Yes, mistress. Sorry, Miss Chloe.'

Her riding whip lashed out, to catch his bare thigh where it showed beneath the hem of his ridiculous frilly skirt. He yelped in pain but didn't drop the drinks, instead passing them to Julian and I as Vanessa carried on.

'You can do better than that, worm.'

'Yes, mistress. Sorry, mistress. I'm very sorry I scared you last night, Miss Chloe, and I'm very sorry I peeped at you in the nude. I'm a miserable peeping Tom and I deserve to be punished.'

Vanessa chuckled.

'And so you shall be. Perhaps I'll even let Chloe whip you? Then again, I suspect you'd enjoy that too much. Now kneel.'

Her last words were sharp and commanding, so much so that I nearly got down myself. Henry obeyed instantly, falling to his knees on the rug between the sofa Julian and I had taken and the comfortable armchair in which Vanessa was seated. She nodded, pleased with his prompt and unquestioning response.

'Face to the floor.'

Again he obeyed, bracing his hands on the rug and lowering his head until his nose was pressed to the floor. His buttocks were lifted, his skirt now well up to reveal frilly white knickers beneath. Vanessa reached out with her riding whip, to tap him gently across both cheeks as she spoke.

'Bare or not, that is the question. I don't suppose Chloe wants to see your scrawny backside, and I certainly don't, but all that froufrou does rather cushion the blows.'

Henry didn't answer, but his face was a picture, full of humiliation and ecstasy at the same time, and so foolish in combination with his maid's outfit that I found myself stifling a giggle, only to realise that I'd probably looked almost as silly bent over Vanessa's knee with my knickers pulled down and my bare bottom stuck in the air while she spanked me. Not quite as ridiculous though, because at least I'd have been able to carry off the maid's uniform. Vanessa still hadn't made up her mind.

'What do you think, Julian, Chloe? Shall we leave the worm the dignity of his frilly knickers, or is the sight of his bottom too horrid?'

Julian made a gesture of casual indifference and Vanessa turned to me. I was already blushing badly, and struggled to speak.

'I ... I don't know. Don't knickers always come down for ... for that sort of thing?'

It was the only thing I could think of to say that would seem remotely appropriate, and it set my blushes hotter still. Vanessa smiled.

'Do knickers always come down? I bet yours do, but then you have a beautiful bottom. Hmm ... perhaps you're right.'

She reached out, to twitch Henry's panties down at the back, exposing two skinny buttocks and drawing a gasp from him, something with which I could entirely sympathise. Vanessa tapped the sting of her whip against his cheeks.

'So then, worm, this is for being a peeping Tom. I think 20 strokes should do it.'

Her riding whip came up, and down, landing across his buttocks with a meaty sound that made my stomach jump

110

and my own cheeks tighten. I was sure it hurt far more than her hand had done, but unlike me he took it well, probably because he was used to it, and he didn't even begin to gasp until the eighth stroke. By 15 he was clutching the rug with his teeth gritted in pain and his eyes tight shut, but Vanessa never even slowed down, laying in each stroke hard and precise across his bottom until she at last reached 20. His cheeks were a mesh of red lines, his skin prickled with sweat and his breathing deep and even, while I could see that his cock had begun to swell and stiffen. Vanessa's voice was rich with contempt as she spoke again.

'And for scaring her, perhaps just another ten. After all, she is a very silly girl, and there's no insult to me, unlike peeping at her!'

On the last word she gave him another stroke, much harder than the last and obviously unexpected. At that he finally cried out, and was mumbling broken apologies and promising to behave better in future. She ignored him, but waited until he'd calmed down a little before administering the remaining nine strokes to leave him in a worse state than before, now with his cock hanging turgid into his lowered panties. Vanessa sat back, smiling.

'That will do, for the time being at least. Now, Chloe, what do you suppose happens next?'

'I ... I don't know. Are you going to make him say thank you?'

'No, dear. That sort of privilege is reserved for pretty little things like you. The worm isn't allowed to touch me.'

'I don't know then.'

'Then I'll tell you. The worm is a cuckold, which means that he likes to watch his mistress with other men – preferably beefy, well-endowed men. Julian has always played the part very well.'

The thought made me shiver, but that was one thing I wasn't going to surrender to her. I tried to make a joke of it.

'He can't do that, not now.'

Vanessa nodded.

'No, which is a pity, and I did hope you might be more flexible. Still, there are alternatives. How do you feel about gay sex?'

'Um ... well, it's OK, but ...'

I stopped, my blushes hotter than ever as I realised the implications of what she was saying. My eyes went to Julian, but he merely gave me an enigmatic smile as Vanessa carried on.

'I do hope you're not going to be a little prude about this too. The thing is that a man, a real man, doesn't much care where he puts his cock, as long as he gets his satisfaction. On the other hand, a grovelling, pathetic little worm isn't fit to put his cock anywhere, except into his own hand and that in private so that nobody else has to watch. What he is fit for, though, is to suck a real man's cock.'

Once more I glanced at Julian, horrified.

'Have you?'

His answer was as casual as it was shocking.

'No, but we used to let him lick my balls while we fucked, with Vanessa on top, you understand.'

I nodded dumbly, but the scene was clear in my mind, Julian lying naked on the bed with Vanessa mounted across his hips, her trim little cheeks spread to show off where his cock went into her open pussy as her grovelling husband licked her lover's balls and her bottom slapped in his face as she rode. Vanessa spoke again, her voice soft and teasing.

'Go on, be wicked. Think how he scared you, and he's going to have to suck your lover's penis to say sorry.'

'Um ... well, maybe, I suppose ... if it's what you all want.'

'Oh it is, Chloe, and while the worm is sucking, you and I can have a little cuddle while we watch. Wouldn't you

112

like that?'

I didn't answer, too shocked to know what to say, but it did occur to me that I'd already licked her, and told Julian I wanted to beforehand. If I could give oral sex to another woman, then it was only fair. It was thrilling too, not for the act, but because in some weird way it made my man the top dog, which was not only exciting but right. I stood up, crossed the room and sat in Vanessa's lap. She gave a little purr and her hand closed on my bottom.

'Good girl. There we are, Julian. Didn't I say she'd play?'

He gave a complacent nod, as cool and calm as ever as he drew down his fly and pulled out his cock and balls. I was staring, no longer even bothering to remember not to gape like a goldfish as he crooked a finger to Henry. So many times I'd sucked his cock, so many times I'd felt him harden in my mouth, and now somebody else was to do it – a man at that. I didn't even feel cheated, although I didn't know why not, but I was filled to the brim with shock and arousal and a sense of pride in his sheer masculinity.

Henry crawled to Julian's feet, his face set in what seemed to be utter misery, but that didn't stop him taking hold of the big pale cock and putting it in his mouth. He began to suck, and to tease Julian's balls, his motions not so much eager as eager to please. Julian simply lay back, idly sipping his gin and tonic, his eyes closed in pleasure for the feel of having his cock sucked, which I suppose is much the same whoever is doing it. Vanessa was less reserved, making the little, pleased purring noise in her throat I'd heard before as she took a grip on the hem of my dress and gave it a meaningful tug.

'Come on, Chloe, don't you think we should give Julian something to watch while he's sucked off? Let's have you showing.'

I let it happen, lifting my bottom to allow her to tug my dress up, first around my waist and then higher still, up under my arms with my breasts bare and nothing but my knickers and shoes on below my naked chest. That condition didn't last long either, Vanessa quickly levering my panties down to my ankles to leave me bare on her lap. She began to explore my body, maybe partly for Julian, but mainly for herself. He'd opened his eyes, smiling as he watched my breasts felt and my nipples brought to erection, my bottom gently smacked and my pussy stroked.

It didn't take me long to give in. Soon my thighs had come open and I was allowing Vanessa free play with my pussy, while when she drew my head down to her mouth I let my lips come open immediately, returning her kiss with near equal passion. By then Julian was hard, his cock rearing from his fly into Henry's mouth, fully erect to another man even if he was watching me groped. Vanessa was watching them too, but she was a great deal more interested in me, her fingers exploring with ever more urgency, probing the hole of my vagina, tickling my anus, while she seemed fascinated by the size and weight of my breasts.

My courage built with my excitement, and I'd soon begun to stroke Vanessa's boobs in turn, each a small, firm mound, very different to my own. We began to kiss again, and I saw that Vanessa had closed her eyes, now taking her pleasure solely in me. I couldn't let go so easily, one eye still fixed on Henry as he sucked my boyfriend's cock, his head now bobbing up and down. His face was still set in what I could have sworn was true and bitter humiliation for all that he was putting everything into what he was doing, not only sucking, but playing with Julian's balls and masturbating him into his mouth.

Julian was watching me, smiling as Vanessa suckled at one of my nipples, and then his face had gone abruptly slack and I realised he had come in Henry's mouth. A hard shiver went through me as I saw, and another as Henry swallowed, both sensations close to orgasm, and with that I gave in completely to my own need. Rising, I'd quickly tugged Vanessa's dress up over her hips and chest, to let me get at her naked breasts and her sex. She had no knickers on, and if she was surprised at my sudden urgency she made no effort to stop me getting what I wanted. Down I went, onto my knees, to bury my face between her thighs, licking up the musky perfume of her pussy as my hands went to relieve my own now desperate need.

She sighed in pleasure as I began to lick and, at the same time, to rub at myself. I was going to come at any moment, and my head was full of filthy thoughts – only not fantasies, but memories: Julian feeding his cock into Henry's mouth, Vanessa stripping me nude from breasts to ankles, the feel of her fingers inside my body, and the sight of my lover's cock jerking into another man's mouth – a man who had swallowed what came out. With that I came, still licking eagerly, but not very skilfully. Vanessa had begun to gasp and push herself into my face, now holding me by the hair, but she hadn't come, and as my own shudders faded she spoke, her voice a hoarse croak.

'Whip the dirty brat, Julian.'

I tried to pull back, terrified of the whip, still coming but already awash with guilt. This time Vanessa's voice was a hiss.

'Hold still, you greedy little slut, and fucking lick! Whip her, Julian!'

I was sobbing into her pussy as I continued to lick, still excited but confused and scared. Vanessa tightened her grip in my hair, holding me firmly in place with my bottom stuck out for the riding whip Julian had now picked up. The sting caught my cheeks, gently, then a little harder, each smack sending a little jolt straight to my sex. I tried to tell myself that it was fair, that I deserved punishment for being so dirty, not just for letting Vanessa have me, but for not even trying to put a stop to what had happened between the four of us.

It worked. I stuck my bottom right out, my cheeks wide, my wet pussy flaunted to Julian and his whip, and incidentally to Henry. The smacks got harder, stinging me as I tongued Vanessa, knowing my ordeal wouldn't be over until she'd come, and no longer sure if I wanted it to be. I caught her by the hips, pulling her forward in the chair so that I could get my face between the cheeks of her bottom and my tongue up her anus where it belonged. Vanessa gave a gasp of surprise and delight and Julian's whip smacked down harder still.

'Dirty brat is about right! I've never known a girl so keen to lick another woman's bottom, isn't that right, Chloe?'

I nodded, my tongue now pushed into the tight star of Vanessa's anus as far as it would go, licking eagerly. Julian laughed to see me so dirty, and suddenly the whip was no longer striking home across my cheeks but between them, the leather sting smacking on my open pussy. Moments later I was coming, pushed over the edge for a second time, beaten to orgasm with my tongue in my mistress's anus and willing to have anything done to me for their pleasure, anything at all.

This time when I'd finished I never really came down, and there was no more than the slightest twinge of guilt as I transferred the attention of my tongue back to Vanessa's cunt. Now I was licking eagerly but carefully, using what skill and imagination I had to give her pleasure and with my bottom well stuck out so that she could watch me beaten. Even then she took her time, holding me firmly in place and rubbing herself into my face until, at last, she came, by which time my bottom was hot and criss-crossed with whip marks, but if I was sore I was also happy.

Chapter Twelve

I EXPECTED TO COME down really badly, but I didn't. Perhaps I was getting used to it, or perhaps it was that before I'd been the only one to behave disgracefully, whereas by letting another man suck him off Julian had broken The Rules big time. The only problem I did have was my smacked bottom, because although the whipping hadn't seemed hard at all while I was getting it, both my cheeks were covered in long red welts and there was no shortage of bruising. I even walked back to the Hall bare bottom, after Vanessa had sweetly rubbed cream into my cheeks. By then it was dark, with the lights along the drive making puddles of illumination and utter darkness beyond, but with Julian by my side and my body still pumped up with adrenaline the night held no fears.

It did in the morning. We got up late after a night of steamy, if rather careful, sex, and after wolfing a plate of bacon and eggs Julian went up to his computer. I knew he was going to check on the Inquisitor's blog, but I didn't expect anything new to be up, not when we'd been in the gatehouse until nearly midnight. Whoever it was would barely have had time to update.

He was obviously dedicated, because I'd barely put the plates into the sink when I heard Julian curse, then call to me.

'Chloe! Come and look at this, the little bastard!'

I ran upstairs, to find him with his chair pushed back from the table as he indicated the screen.

'Look!'

I looked. There we were, a good clear shot this time, walking hand in hand up the drive towards the Hall, clearly illuminated by one of the lights, Julian in his baggy combat trousers and loose top, me stark naked except for my heels, my bare bum stripy with whip cuts.

'Shit! He must have been right behind us!'

'That or he's got a seriously expensive lens, and a good camera. That's not even a long exposure, but read this.'

He did so himself, not bothering to wait.

'"There was a ritual last night. I don't know what happened because it was indoors, but there was a lot of screaming and when the girl and her boyfriend left it was obvious she'd been whipped. Just look at the pic! (Fuck me, but she's got a nice arse!) I reckon she got 11 cuts, and 11 is the essence of all that is sinful, harmful and imperfect, as we all know, so if that doesn't prove what they're up to, nothing will!"'

'Bloody hell! He's nuts, but what's 11 got to do with anything?'

'I don't know, presumably it has some occult significance, but I'm sure I gave you more than 11 strokes.'

'More like 20, look.'

I turned my back and pulled my nightie up, allowing him to make a quick count of the welts on my bum.

'19, I think. Some overlap. More than 11 anyway, but that's good. The more he's able to delude himself, the more convincing we'll seem.'

'Do you really want a nutter like that running about the estate?'

'Yes. He's exactly what we need. Look, he's starting to get comments.'

There were only five, and three of those remarked on my bum, with one stating that if he'd been in Julian's place he'd have given me a much harder whipping and then buggered me.

'What a pervert!'

Julian merely laughed, then clicked on a link attached to the next comment, which was by somebody calling himself "Triplesix" and approved of what we'd done, accusing the Inquisitor of trying to interfere with the valid expression of our beliefs. The website was dedicated to the occult, and specifically to Aleister Crowley – pretty hysterical stuff but with a forum boasting over 10,000 members. Julian drew a deep sigh.

'We're in! They'll be queuing past Norwich, especially if they think they might catch a glimpse of you getting a whacking.'

I didn't answer, thinking of 10,000 people looking at my smacked bottom. And I'd meant to keep my new-found taste for being spanked a secret. Now everybody from the village to Vancouver could see that I got it, and I was sure it wouldn't be long before the picture was all over the net. The only mercy was that it didn't show my face, but that was small consolation. It was still me, still my naked body marked by Vanessa's whip, on show to men by their million; frustrated teenagers surfing for porn, dirty old men, students in their college rooms, American nerds, Japanese boys with a taste for the weird, men in Bangkok and Berlin, New Delhi and New York, all ogling my body, thinking of my pain and humiliation, some of them masturbating, the one who'd made the comment imagining me whipped harder still as he eased his cock up my bottom. A powerful shiver ran down my spine at the thought and I felt my anus tighten, but Julian was already rising from the chair.

'We don't want to put him off, but I do want to know more about him and how he works. How come we didn't see him last night, for example? Let's see if we can work out where he was when he took the photograph.'

'What if he's watching us now?'

'This was posted less than half an hour ago. If he sees

us and comments that tells us a lot.'

I nodded, unable to deny the logic of what he was saying.

Even fully dressed I felt exposed as we walked down the drive, Julian holding a print-out of the photograph the Inquisitor had taken. It was easy to work out which light we'd been under, as there were only four and the Hall showed faintly in the background. We stopped underneath it, Julian frowning at the picture.

'Yes, we were here, definitely. OK, stay here.'

I did as I was told, watching as he walked towards the gatehouse. The drive curved slightly, but when he reached the gate itself I could still see him, peering out from the shelter of one of the tall brick pillars. If that was where the Inquisitor had been hiding then we'd passed just feet away as we left the gatehouse, almost close enough to touch. Julian was walking back, looking pleased with himself.

'That's where he was, and it means we're looking for somebody with a good DSLR and an expensive lens, quite a long one too. Let's set a trap.'

'How?'

'We'll advertise a special tour, something that's bound to attract his interest.'

'What, like seeing me get a whipping?'

'Don't tempt me. I'd love to spank you in front of a group of visitors. But seriously, we do need to give him an opportunity he can't refuse.'

'He seems to be into rituals. Maybe if we say we're going to re-create one of John Aylsham's ones?'

'Great idea! We'll start with the first ones, which were quite simple – a sort of reversal of Holy Communion if I'm thinking of the right one. Come, library.'

We hurried back, both full of mischief as we returned to the Hall. There were quite a few valuable books in the library and it was generally kept locked. I'd only glanced in before, when he was showing me around, and had never really had a chance to take it in. It was a big square room, occupying the corner of the house at the far end to our bedrooms so that the high windows with their lead panes and panels of old green glass illuminated the table at the centre of the room in morning sunlight but left the bookcases in relative shade. The cases were high, reaching almost to the ceiling, and there was an ancient wooden ladder mounted on wheels that Julian used to climb to the shelf where John Aylsham's diaries were kept.

I'd been expecting barely legible script peppered with lots of "ye"s and "thou"s, but both his hand and his language were surprisingly clear. So was his logic, at least from the point of view of an educated man living in the late 17th century, as Julian explained.

'The important thing is to realise that he actually believed in God and the Devil. This was two centuries before Darwin, after all, and even Newton did as much work on theology as he did on physics, so when John Aylsham invented this ritual, he wasn't playing, like just about anybody who did it nowadays would be. He expected it to work.'

He had the book open, treating it with exaggerated care as he turned the pages one by one and carrying on when he had the passage he wanted.

'Here we are, "*To partake of the sacrament is to become one with Christ and so it must be that to reverse the sacrament is to become one with the Devil. How then to reverse the sacrament?*" The next bit is quite involved, quoting all the sources he'd read, mainly Paracelsus, who was a Renaissance occultist, or other people who'd drawn on Paracelsus for their own ideas. The symbols you draw on your body come from his book, by the way.'

'You mean they're real?'

'As real as any of this stuff is. Anyway, John goes on for quite a bit, but it all seems to come down to what to use as a substitute for communion bread and wine. That was the basis of the first few rituals, the idea being that he'd summon the Devil into the body of one of his acolytes and could then strike his bargain. He tried various things, some of them pretty gross, but let's see ...'

Again he began to turn the pages, as carefully as before, his finger flicking to the relevant parts of the text. He hadn't been joking about the substitutions being gross.

'I'm not drinking pee, or pig's blood, and I'm certainly not eating ...'

'Relax. We're only doing this for the Inquisitor. We can fake it.'

'Good! But we'll have visitors around us, won't we?'

'Yes. A pity really, as that means you can't be naked.'

'Are you sure he'll even come? He'll know it's not the real thing after all.'

'He'll come if he knows you're going to be in a bikini, and I intend to put a photo on the Hall website with the announcement – nothing too kinky, just enough to arouse his interest.'

We spent the next couple of hours setting up our trap. I got into my black bikini and sat on the altar in a mildly provocative pose, allowing Julian to photograph me. The picture went on the website, along with an announcement that we would be reproducing one of Sir John Aylsham's original satanic rituals on the following Sunday. That would mean we got a lot of people, making it easier for the Inquisitor to blend in with the crowd, but because of that he was more likely to come and Julian was still confident of being able to identify him without scaring him off.

I felt both nervous and excited, while it was hard to forget what an exhibition I'd made of myself – or rather, what an exhibition the Inquisitor had made of me. It was a turn-on, no question, but I could have cheerfully strangled him, probably before bringing myself to orgasm over the thought of all those thousands of male – and maybe female

– eyes lingering over the contours of my body – and, in particular, my smacked bottom.

We had to square our decision with Vanessa, but she readily agreed, as always more than happy to give Julian free rein with anything designed to bring in more visitors. She had also changed her attitude to me, now more open and less condescending, although still superior. Henry was also with her when we went over to the gatehouse, and he could barely bring himself to meet my eyes. Vanessa thought it was funny and began to tease him, which might well have led to something had not Julian and I needed to greet the day's tourists.

It seemed quite likely that the Inquisitor would be among them, and we kept a careful watch as we went through the now familiar routine. Julian had warned me not to rely on preconceptions of what the man might look like, but it was hard as I had a clear image in my head. He would be of middling height or rather less, overweight if not actually obese, probably bearded and sloppily dressed. It also seemed likely that he would be on his own, or at least not part of one of the families who made up the bulk of our visitors.

There were 13 in the tour, and one of them drew my attention even as we watched them assemble from the churchyard. He was in a group of three – all young men – and they didn't seem to know each other particularly well so might even have met on the bus. At least three inches shorter than me, he was even smaller than I'd imagined, and also distinctly fat. He had no beard, but he did carry an obviously expensive Canon camera with a telephoto lens. Julian didn't seem to have noticed so I drew his attention.

'What about the guy in the baggy combat trousers and the red T-shirt, the fat one?'

'Could be, I suppose, but why's he more likely than the two standing with him, or the old man sitting on the bench?'

'He's got a good camera, for a start.'

'It's a Canon. The Inquisitor mentioned a D90, which is a Nikon.'

'Oh. Maybe he has two?'

Julian made a doubtful face, but I wasn't to be put off so easily.

'I don't think it's the others anyway. I can't see the old guy creeping around the grounds in the middle of the night, and the other two are really quite good looking.'

'What's that got to do with it?'

'Well, the Inquisitor's sure to be a bit of a loner, isn't he? Not that good with girls, still single in his 30s, probably still lives with his mum.'

'You're thinking of psychopaths.'

'And the sort of guy who's into conspiracy theories and stuff.'

'Maybe.'

'Anyway, let's keep an eye on him, and I think you should follow him after the tour.'

'Me?'

'I can't, can I? What if he turns nasty?'

'Run away. I mean, he's not going anywhere very fast, is he?'

'Still ...'

I trailed off, actually rather keen on the idea of trying to follow somebody, and it was hard to be scared by the dumpy little man who was now poking about in his ear in an absent-minded fashion. Julian glanced at his watch.

'Come on, let's go. Your turn.'

We stepped forward, as always emerging from the lych gate as suddenly and mysteriously as possible. I was in my black dress as usual, but I'd refined my make-up to add to the effect, and I could now deliver my lines with the same fluid ease as Julian.

'Ladies, gentlemen, welcome to Candle Street Hall.'

They'd all turned to me, and to Julian, who had stepped

out behind me. I began to go into the legend of Black Dog Lane, all the while trying to work out if my suspect was behaving oddly in any way and quickly deciding that he was. He stayed at the back, for one thing, as if trying to hide behind his taller friends, and he kept taking pictures, not just of the sights but of me and Julian. As we walked up Black Dog Lane he was well behind the rest of the group and appeared to be studying the ground, presumably in the hope of finding some tracks. At the Hall he was worse, distinctly nervous and far more interested in his surroundings than in what we were saying. He also seemed unusually interested in me, which I pointed out to Julian the moment I had a chance.

'That man's been staring at me all day!'

'So what? He's a human male, isn't he? Although in your case I'm sure a chimpanzee ...'

'Stop being silly. I'm sure it's him – the Inquisitor.'

'In that case don't draw attention to yourself.'

'I won't.'

I'd have gone on, but an elderly American couple were approaching us, wanting to know the juicy details of Lady Howard's crime and whether or not they'd be able to see the coach of bones if they paid extra. Julian was always better at tackling that sort of question, so I left him to it, grouping the others together to tell them they were free to explore the grounds until we closed. I was careful not to pay any extra attention to my suspect, and made a point of joining a family to show them where Sir Richard Aylsham had fought a duel with Charles James Fox.

By the time I'd finished Julian was still with the two Americans and there was no sign of my suspect. The two men he'd been with were visible though, sitting on the edge of the bank sharing water from a bottle. There was a chance the man was indoors, so I made a hasty survey of the rooms, only to glance from the window of one of the show bedrooms and find him standing at the mouth of the folly path. He was looking at the ground, his camera in his hands. I had my proof.

I hurried downstairs, eager to find Julian, but he was nowhere to be seen. Moving through to the kitchen, I peered out. My suspect was gone, but I was pretty sure of the direction he'd taken. With my heart in my mouth I ran for the folly path, moving cautiously on into the woods. Close to the folly itself I took cover behind a big straggling holly, allowing me to see into the folly itself. He was there, actually inside the folly, beside the altar where Julian had laid me for sex so many times. In his hand was a sheep's skull.

He was the Inquisitor, there was no doubt at all in my mind. His appearance, his behaviour, the camera – everything fitted, which just went to show that my intuition was worth more than Julian's logic. Now all I had to do was find out who he was and where he lived to ensure that we were fully in control. If he'd booked online or by post Graham would already have his details, and he'd had his ticket in advance so, unless he'd paid cash at the gatehouse, we had him.

I should have left. We now had everything we needed to identify him, almost certainly, and the sensible thing would have been to back off and let him think he hadn't been spotted. I couldn't do it. My adrenaline was running high and it was impossible to be scared of a man who looked like a garden gnome. Anyway, he wasn't paying the slightest attention to me, fascinated by the altar as he photographed the skulls and the candles, the pot of wax and the outline of the pentagram.

My best moment came when he realised the significance of the stain. He'd been very serious, his face set in a frown of concentration as he photographed each detail of our fake ritual, only to suddenly stop, his mouth dropping slowly open as the implications of the marks on the altar top sank in. For me it was a beautiful moment of exhibitionist fantasy, for all that he couldn't actually see me at all.

That didn't matter. He could see that a woman had been fucked on the altar, he could guess why and he could guess it was me. All afternoon he'd been staring at my tits, no doubt undressing me in his mind, and no doubt ogling the way my bum showed beneath my dress with the same lewd interest when my back was to him. Now he'd be imagining me, naked, my body laid out on the altar, so turned on by Julian that I was not just dripping juice, but running juice. I could feel his envy, his arousal, and as he made a hasty adjustment to his crotch, I knew that my thoughts were more than just idle speculation.

I was sure he'd have had enough, with so many incriminating shots in the bag, while he was clearly badly in need of an orgasm. That was funny, disgusting but funny, imagining him pulling at his weedy little cock – and I couldn't imagine it as anything but little and weedy – while his head was full of thoughts of my naked or near-naked body, laid out on the altar for fucking, or bent down for my bottom to be whipped, or mounted by Julian on the moonlit lawn.

Had I been him I'd have done it then and there if I'd been sure I was safe, or hurried home, or, most likely, found somewhere quiet to relieve my tension. He went for the third option, throwing a last guilty glance around the interior of the folly and then starting down the bank. As he crossed the field he was walking fast, and there was nothing I could do but watch and wait, knowing that if I followed him before he reached the reed beds I was sure to be seen.

That gave him a long start, but when he finally disappeared I was running immediately. Again, I knew I should have turned back, but the whole situation was too good to miss. The thought of him masturbating was disgusting, but it was also funny, and most importantly I had my phone on me so I would be able to take a picture of him and post it on the web to give him a taste of his own medicine. I was also grateful for the phone because it meant I could call Julian and tell him what was going on once I'd reached the river bank. He laughed when I said I thought the Inquisitor was going off to wank over me among the reeds, and promised to follow.

Now fully confident, I began to pick my way along the duckboard path, very slowly and stopping to listen despite being fairly sure where the Inquisitor would go: either the old boathouse or Henry's hide. If Henry was around he might be in for a shock, but that made no real difference to me, while if I ran into the Inquisitor I could always act the officious staff member and point out that when we said he could wander around the grounds at will, that did not include masturbating in the reed beds.

He wasn't in the boathouse, and I moved on more cautiously than ever, not quite sure how to get to the hide, but knowing the path to it had to join my own at some point. It had grown very quiet, and my nerves were beginning to get to me again, making me wonder if I should wait for Julian, but as I came around a corner the duckboards gave way to a path of pressed earth along the top of a low bank fringed with willows and oaks. At the far end was the Inquisitor, three-quarters turned away from me. He appeared to be taking pictures of the stems of the reeds at the bottom of the bank.

I nipped quickly back, puzzled by his behaviour, but only for a moment. Evidently he'd found a footprint, probably Henry's, and was photographing it in order to compare the pattern of the shoe sole with those he'd taken pictures of on the estate. He was certainly thorough, and that meant his camera would be full of pictures – incriminating pictures – perhaps even including the ones he's taken of me and Julian walking back from the gatehouse. At the thought of him taking sneaky pictures of me in the nude I forgot all about letting him get on with his snooping for the sake of our publicity. It was just too much, that this little runt of a man had the cheek to come creeping around taking pictures while I enjoyed myself with my boyfriend, and from what he'd said on his blog it was quite obvious he got off on them. At the very least he'd have pictures of me from earlier in the afternoon, no doubt taken to make the best of my figure. Letting men see me when I was in control of the situation was one thing, being peeped at quite another, especially when he'd broadcast a picture of me with a freshly whipped bottom to effectively the entire world. I stepped out from cover, striding towards him.

'Give me that!'

He looked up, surprised. I repeated my order.

'Give me that camera, now!'

'Why?'

'You know perfectly well why, you dirty little pervert!'

'What do you mean? You've got this all wrong!'

'Oh I have, have I? Let's see the pictures you've been taking then.'

'Sure.'

It was not the answer I'd been expecting, and it rather took the wind out of my sails. Julian appeared at that moment, coming up behind us and immediately taking charge of the situation.

'What's going on? Chloe?'

He didn't sound best pleased, reminding me that I'd promised to hold back.

'I'm sorry, Julian, but I just wanted to teach the dirty little peeping Tom a lesson.'

'I'm not a peeping Tom! I was taking pictures of snails, that's all!'

'Snails?! Yeah, sure you were.'

'Yes, snails. I'm a malacologist.'

'A what?'

'Somebody who studies molluscs. I've just completed

129

my PhD on the gastropod fauna of the Norfolk Broads, which is unique. Look.'

He'd moved the camera towards us and switched to display mode. The screen showed a small, gelatinous-looking snail climbing the stem of a reed.

'This is *Succinea putris,* and this one is *Oxyloma pfeifferi.*'

It was another snail, much like the first, but I wasn't falling for such an obvious diversion.

'Keep going.'

'OK. These are *Planorbarius corneus*, the Great Ramshorn, up by the river, and ...'

He carried on, showing snail after snail after snail, some among the reeds, others in the woods by the Hall. There were also some of the Hall, and of Julian and I, but nothing even remotely suggestive, never mind the sort of thing a voyeur would want. Finally he returned to the original snail.

'You see, just snails, and a few I took on your tour.'

There wasn't really much I could say.

'Oh. Sorry.'

Julian was trying not to laugh, which wasn't really very helpful. The snail man put away his camera, his voice surprisingly mild considering I'd just accused him of being a pervert.

'I'm sorry if you got the wrong idea. People do sometimes.'

'No, really, it was my fault.'

We lapsed into an embarrassed silence, broken by Julian.

'I'm Julian d'Alveda, by the way. This is my girlfriend, Chloe Anthony.'

'Ian Dobson. Hi.'

He had extended one pudgy hand, which Julian shook, then carried on, his voice as calm and matter of fact as ever.

'Tell me, Ian, do you feel that Chloe was rude to you?'

'Er ... a little perhaps, but it's not important.'

'On the contrary. You are a paying customer and deserve to be treated with respect. Possibly you might even feel that she should be punished in some way?'

The snail man just looked puzzled and a little embarrassed, but I could see the way the conversation was going and I recognised the light, amused tone in Julian's voice.

'Julian, no ...'

'Be quiet, Chloe. Ian, would you like to watch Chloe spanked?'

'What?!'

'Would you like to watch Chloe spanked? I think it's only suitable, when she was so rude to you, and it's only fair that you be allowed to watch. It would do her the world of good too – both the spanking and having you watch, that is.'

My mouth had come open in wordless protest and the blood had rushed to my cheeks, for all I knew that he was only joking, or at least I hoped he was. Yet if I was embarrassed the snail man was no better, his face red and his mouth working as he struggled for something to say. Finally I found my voice.

'Julian! That's not funny!'

'It's not supposed to be funny, Chloe. Now come on, you know it's what you need.'

As he spoke he'd taken my wrist, pulling me towards where the branch of a willow made the perfect seat, just right for him to put me over his knee. I was still fairly sure he wouldn't go through with it – not all the way – but I was already completely mortified and couldn't help but protest.

'Julian!'

'Come on, Chloe, don't make a fuss. You'll only embarrass yourself. You're due a spanking, and that's that.'

131

He was still pulling, and I didn't have the strength to resist him, either mentally or physically. The snail man was just standing there, gaping like a fish as I was pulled up the bank, still trying to protest but only managing nervous laughter, which broke to a wail of dismay as I was taken firmly down across his legs. At that I realised that I was really going to be spanked, and in front of the snail man, who looked horrified but showed no inclination to be a gentleman and spare my blushes. I couldn't stop it, and deep inside I knew it was exactly what I needed, but that didn't stop me from babbling objections as Julian made himself comfortable.

'Not in front of him, Julian, please! Do it at home, if you have to, but not here! Please, Julian, I'll be good, I promise! Julian!'

My final word came out as a squeal, because he'd applied a single firm pat to the seat of my dress, then another and it had begun, my first true punishment spanking, a thought that filled me with such agonising humiliation that what little fight I had left just vanished. I stopped struggling, to hang limp and pathetic across his legs, my bottom lifted to his hand as he continued to spank me, his voice now cool and even as he spoke.

'Good girl, Chloe. That's right, you know this is what you deserve.'

All I could manage in response was a weak shake of my head, my resistance crushed by his masterful manner and my own need, but I didn't realise that he'd only just begun. After maybe a couple of dozen swats he stopped and spoke once more.

'Let's do this properly, with your dress up.'

'No!'

I snatched back, but Julian was ready for me, catching my wrist and twisting it up into the small of my back, trapping me. Still I struggled, wriggling crazily and pleading with him not to lift my dress, but to no avail as it

132

was hauled high, right up onto my back to leave the seat of my panties bulging out behind me in full view of the goggling snail man. Again Julian began to spank me, harder now and aiming where my flesh stuck out at the sides of my knickers, to make my cheeks bounce and turn my pleas and sobs to gasps of pain. As he spanked he continued to talk, as calm as ever, as if smacking his girlfriend's panty-clad bottom in front of a complete stranger was the most natural thing in the world.

'I really am very sorry she was so rude to you, Ian, but I do hope this makes up for it? And she does have a lovely bottom, doesn't she? So cheeky, but wonderfully firm. In fact, why don't I pull her panties down and let you see her properly.'

'Julian!'

My scream rang out loud and long, but it was too late. He hadn't even given me a chance to protest, but simply whipped my knickers down at the back, leaving not just most of my bum cheeks on show, but every rude detail between, including my anus and my embarrassingly wet pussy. I felt the sudden cold from my juices as the air touched my sex, and even smelt my own excitement. Julian merely laughed and spoke again.

'Stop making such a fuss, Chloe. A girl's knickers should always come down when she's spanked, you said so yourself.'

The best I could manage in response was a sob, because I had said exactly that, and I knew that if he hadn't pulled my knickers down I wouldn't have felt I'd been spanked properly. As it was I was bare, my bottom nude to the man I'd been rude to, my penance as much the exposure of my pussy and anus as my pain. That was fair, but what wasn't fair was the state of my sex, and I was praying the snail man hadn't noticed, but not even that intimate detail was to be left private. The spanking stopped. Julian's hand delved between my cheeks and my vagina had been spread for inspection. Another sob escaped my lips, more heartfelt than before, but Julian's voice was still cool and level as he addressed the snail man.

'She gets very excited when I spank her. It turns her on like nothing else. Not that she can help it, but that doesn't mean it's not a real punishment, does it, darling?'

I didn't answer, too angry, too humiliated, but most of all, too aroused. Julian carried on with my spanking, but he wasn't prepared to accept my silence, demanding a response.

'Come on, darling, answer me! Is this a real punishment?'

He began to spank harder, perhaps mistaking my speechless humiliation for obstinacy, and after a moment the words were spilling from my mouth in between gasps and yelps.

'Yes! It's a real punishment ... a proper punishment, and I deserve it!'

I'd said it, and I meant it, but the emotion of acknowledging my own feelings was too much for me. My eyes went misty and I'd started to cry, at which Julian stopped immediately, to pull me up and take me in his arms, cuddling me as I let my emotions out in a great flood of tears. He held on, whispering into my ear to soothe me until, at last, I had calmed down enough to remember that we had an audience, my blushes rising hot once more as I turned to where the snail man had watched my spanking.

He had fled, perhaps able to cope with the thoroughly rude display of my bottom as I was spanked but not with the far more intimate display of emotion I'd given when I broke down. It was just as well he'd gone too, because Julian had taken me to that special place where normal conventions simply don't matter, and being watched wouldn't have stopped me as I went down on my knees to free my lover's cock from his trousers and take it in my mouth.

Julian accepted what I was doing as his due, stroking my hair as I sucked on his cock, which was already more than half hard. It was all I wanted, just to be allowed to pleasure him in return for my punishment, but I was his completely, to do with as he pleased. When he took a firm grip in my hair and pulled me off his prick I didn't resist, nor as he stood up to ease me gently into position over the willow branch. My dress came up once more to leave my bare red bottom thrust out towards the empty fens and I was ready for whatever treatment he chose to give me. I thought he'd fuck me from behind, maybe after a good whipping with twigs from the willow tree, but as I felt the head of his cock press between my bottom cheeks I realised he had something else in mind. He was going to bugger me.

I just hung my head, completely surrendered to him, even as I felt his cock touch my anus, knowing he'd put it right up and deal with me properly, just as he always did. It wasn't easy, my mouth wide and my breath coming in sharp, urgent gasps as he pushed himself gradually up my bottom. My hands were clutched tight to the rough bark of the willow branch, my body shaking, with fresh tears rolling down my cheeks, but I wanted it, and when at last I felt his balls squash to the flesh of my vacant sex and knew he was all in, my sigh held as much pleasure as relief.

He began to push inside me, slowly at first and then faster, until the hard muscles of his belly were slapping against my hot bottom cheeks. I took it as best I could, dizzy with reaction and lost in an ecstasy that came as much from my surrender as the motion of his cock in my bottom hole, but when he reached under my belly to find my sex and began to rub my body took over in an instant. A few light touches to my clit and I was there, coming in a welter of dirty ecstasy so good I screamed out his name, begging him to bugger me harder and promising to be his for ever until my words gave way to a shriek, then another, as he gave a single rough grunt and I realised he'd come.

I was biting my lip as he withdrew, which was what made me raise my head just in time to catch a glint off among the reeds. Instantly I thought of the snail man and light reflected from the glass of a lens, but there was nothing I could do until Julian was free of my body, leaving me babbling and kicking my feet in panic until I was finally able to get up. I jerked my dress down in a pointless attempt to cover my modesty, but my sense of utter abandonment had fled.

Julian had also seen the flash of light and was scanning the sea of reeds all around us. I could see all the way back to the folly, where a distant figure in a red top could only be the snail man. He was walking along the bank, in quite a different direction, and I began to wonder if all I'd seen was a reflection of sun on water. Then came the sound of an outboard engine, coughing to life just yards away, where tall reeds hid the open water of a minor channel. Julian rushed forward, barging through the undergrowth, only to break out in time to see a punt pull out from among the reeds. In it was seated a man in combats with a camera slung around his neck. He turned, saw us, the look of triumph on his face changed to shock, then, as he realised he was safe, to dirty, lust-filled glee.

Chapter Thirteen

THE MAN WHO CALLED himself the Inquisitor had watched me and Julian having sex, and no ordinary sex. His blog confirmed it the next day, with my blushes growing hotter by the moment as I read what he'd uploaded.

"Another encounter! There were three of them this time. They'd been in the folly, and must have been conducting a ritual, or perhaps preparing for one, but I didn't get close enough to see what was going on until later. The girl, who calls herself Chloe, was arguing with a man I'd not seen before. I couldn't hear at all clearly, but I did catch several arcane terms. Julian d'Alveda himself then appeared and demanded that the strange man show some photographs he had on his camera. He did, and while I do not know what those photographs showed they mollified the girl, making it evident to her that she had been in the wrong.

"Julian d'Alveda then spanked her. Yes, I mean it, an old-fashioned spanking, across his knee with her bottom bare while the other man watched, something possible only among a group of exceptional intimacy and very odd moral standards, but when you worship Satan I suppose that sort of thing is only to be expected. So is what happened afterwards, because when the third man had left it became obvious that Chloe was excited by her punishment, a true daughter of the Devil! She not only sucked D'Alveda's cock, but bent over for him to give her anal sex."

That was it, a hurried entry no doubt written immediately on his return, but he'd taken the time to post some pictures; one of the three of us together, another of me over Julian's knee with my legs kicking and my bare red bottom on full show, and a third worse still, of Julian easing his erection between my bottom cheeks and my face set in abandoned ecstasy. I could only stare, silent as I took in the awful details of what had been two of the most intimate and intense moments of my life, a spanking in front of a stranger and having my anal virginity taken.

I am an exhibitionist, but this took showing off to a whole new level, robbing me of every scrap of dignity, every last vestige of privacy and mystery, but while I was truly appalled I could feel my arousal bubbling up inside me. It was so strong I felt weak and collapsed back onto Julian's bed, not sure if I wanted to scream in mortification or stick my hands down my panties and bring myself to orgasm.

Julian didn't seem to mind at all, delighted with the extra publicity the posting was sure to draw for Candle Street Hall and apparently oblivious to the violation of his own privacy, and mine. Only when I sat down did he react, joining me on the bed to fold me in his arms and kiss me gently on the forehead. At that I gave way, unable to hold back for all my outrage, responding to Julian's kiss and letting my thighs slip apart as I lay back on the bed.

He got the message, as always, his hand sliding between my legs as he gathered me in to kiss and caress my body. I was feeling deeply ashamed of myself even as my panties were pulled aside and his fingers entered my body, but I couldn't stop myself, allowing him to pull my dress high to bare my breasts, to kiss and touch where he wanted until my legs were wide apart in urgent need. He mounted me, pulling his cock from his fly and rubbing it in the wetness of my sex to make himself hard, then slipping up inside me.

I closed my eyes as he began to fuck me, thinking of how I'd looked, first spanked and then buggered, the one in front of another man for my deliberate humiliation, the other supposedly private, but both witnessed by the Inquisitor and posted on the net for all the world to see. At that thought my body gave a little jerk, and again as I ran the awful thought through my head, with Julian's cock pumping faster and faster inside me as I revelled in my own shame. I was going to come, and that knowledge in itself made my feelings stronger still, to think of myself coming to orgasm over the thoughts of thousands upon thousands of people gloating over the sight of me being spanked and then buggered.

The tears were rolling from my eyes as I came, but it was bliss, long and sweet and hard, giving way not to guilt or self-recrimination but a strange, helpless feeling as Julian clung tight to my body until he had finished himself inside me. Even then we stayed together, neither speaking as I clung to him with a need more desperate than ever before, and as my muddled senses slowly came back together I realised that not only was I completely in love with him but I depended on him to hold me together.

We walked over to the gatehouse hand in hand, Julian as calm as ever as we discussed the situation and how to make the best of it, although I was more interested in the Inquisitor.

'Do you think he'll be back?'

'I don't see how he could keep away. I know I couldn't. He'll be cautious though, now that we've seen him. I shouldn't have chased him, really, but I reacted by instinct.'

'He knows who we are, so he must have been on a tour, but I didn't recognise him. He has to be fairly local too, doesn't he, to come and go like that?'

'Maybe, but he could come from as far away as London or Birmingham, if he's obsessive enough. Not that it matters, as long as he keeps giving us plenty of free publicity.'

It mattered to me, although I wasn't sure why when the damage was already done, save that even though Julian and I had set the man up, and despite my reaction to his behaviour, I still wanted to confront him. Julian would have been sympathetic but wouldn't have understood, so I kept quiet.

At the gatehouse Graham gave us an unusually cheerful 'Good morning' and we went upstairs, to where Vanessa had her feet up with a steaming cup of coffee in one hand. I could hear the sound of Henry cleaning from another room, but nobody took any notice as Vanessa greeted us, kissing Julian and planting a firm slap across my bottom. She'd been looking at her computer screen, with the Inquisitor's blog still up, and she was smiling as she spoke.

'You're a little tart, Chloe. It's just as well that you enjoy being spanked, isn't it, because nobody has ever deserved it as much as you do. Well done, Julian, but I hope you can cope this Sunday, because we currently have 157 people booked.'

I'd started to go red again at the way she'd been speaking to me, and my blush grew hotter still at the thought of conducting a tour that would undoubtedly include people who'd seen not only my whipped bottom after the earlier incident, but Julian dealing with me out in the reed beds. It wasn't fair to give Julian all the credit either, when I'd been so deeply involved, effectively sacrificing my dignity for the sake of her business. I wanted to tell her that I wasn't a tart, and to attempt to explain my muddled feelings, but I knew she'd just laugh and kept quiet as Julian responded to her.

'That's fine, although not all of them will be able to visit the folly at the same time. What I suggest we do is to set up the folly as if in the middle of one of John Aylsham's rituals, perhaps with Chloe on the altar, although that would mean you'd have to help with the tour?'

Vanessa raised one haughty eyebrow at the thought of being expected to do some work. Julian merely shrugged.

'Unless you'd prefer to be on the altar?'

'Don't be impudent. Very well, I'll help, and I suppose Henry's capable of shepherding people about, but you'll need to do the talking.'

'Of course. I'll bring the tourists down to the folly in batches, and if they miss their turn, that's their problem, because what really matters is what happens *after* they've left.'

'Which is?'

'The Inquisitor will be watching, probably from a safe distance, but I don't see how he can stay away. That's why, once the grounds are clear, we continue with the ritual, as if we were doing it for real. In fact we will be, to all intents and purposes, or at least it will look as if we are to the Inquisitor. Ideally it ought to look as if it works too, but we'd need somebody who can pretend he's become possessed by the Devil.'

'You would seem to be the ideal candidate.'

'No, because I have to take John Aylsham's role. Do you think Henry could pull it off?'

Vanessa's answering laugh was pure scorn.

'The worm? He'd be better as the sacrifice.'

I'd been struggling to pull up the full details of John Aylsham's rituals from my memory, but I wasn't sure which one Julian was referring to and broke in with a question.

'Hang on – if I'm the sacrifice, what happens to me?'

Julian grinned.

'You get fucked by the Devil.'

'Meaning Henry?'

Vanessa laughed, but Julian at least had the decency to look slightly abashed. I went on quickly while I had at least some advantage.

141

'I'm sorry, but that's asking too much. I ... I don't mind having dirty things done to me, but it has to be by you, Julian, and ... maybe Vanessa if it's spanking and ...'

I'd grown crimson with embarrassment as I spoke, because they both knew exactly what I meant and Vanessa's mouth was curled up into a small smile, registering both amusement and contempt. After a moment of awkward silence she spoke up.

'Does it really matter? One more cock? I bet you've had plenty, haven't you?'

I forced myself to look her in the face, but I was struggling to keep my voice even as I replied.

'Yes, it does matter, and no, not all that many. Sorry, Julian, but ...'

He lifted a hand. 'Fair enough, I respect your limits. How about you then, Vanessa?'

'Allow the worm to have me? You are joking, aren't you?'

I couldn't help but point something out. 'He is your husband, Vanessa.'

'He's a worm, and barely fit to lick my boots. You don't understand our relationship, Chloe.'

I was fairly sure I did, or at least that I was beginning to, but I shut up as Julian went on, his voice now firm.

'We need to get it done, convincingly, but the more unconventional it is the more the Inquisitor will be impressed and the more he'll write. Vanessa will have to take on the role of the possessed servant and Henry can help out with menial tasks. Is that acceptable?'

He was looking at me, his eyes boring into mine and I'd nodded before I could think twice. Vanessa had no qualms at all, reaching out to run a slow hand over the curve of my bottom as she replied.

'Oh yes, that's acceptable. In fact that's ideal. How would it be if I sat on the little tart's face?'

A powerful shiver ran through my body at her words,

but I couldn't help but protest.

'He'll be taking photographs, which he'll put up on the net!'

Vanessa laughed once more as she gestured at her computer screen, where the picture of Julian easing his erection between the cheeks of my bottom was still up.

'Would they be any worse than that?'

I could only hang my head in defeat, too weak to resist the idea of having a picture of her sitting on my face as I licked added to the gallery of my shame – and, in all honesty, too thrilled.

By the Sunday morning the number of people booked for the tour had risen past the 200 mark. That included two coaches chartered by a paranormal society none of us had ever heard of and the representatives of no less than seven other groups as well as the merely curious and the usual compliment of tourists. I'd been feeling slightly stunned by the whole thing as well as embarrassed at the thought of what they'd almost certainly seen, but on the day I found myself so busy I had no time for anything but work.

We opened with the usual tour, Julian and I taking a group each while Vanessa dealt with the stragglers and Graham manned the office. Henry was also there, but was simply too shy and reserved to be any real use and Vanessa had soon sent him down to the temple to make sure the preparations we'd made the evening before weren't interfered with. I was having trouble myself, with the sheer numbers and because many of them knew a great deal more about Black Shuck and Lady Howard than I did myself. There were even questions about the low-frequency vibration effect, which I answered evasively, and about John Aylsham's rituals, which I put off.

By the time we were ready to move on to the folly I was glad to be able to give over my responsibilities in favour of merely lying on the stone slab, and it was really quite amusing to watch Vanessa growing increasingly flustered as she struggled to make so many people do as she wanted. Julian was cooler by far, his voice loud but calm as he gave instructions but quite indifferent to those few who wandered off. Soon he had the first group down at the folly, standing around it and peering in at me where I lay on the slab. I was at the centre of a pentagram, each corner marked out with a sheep's skull on which stood a black candle with the dark wax already running down over the pale bone. A brass chafing dish stood to one side, along with various other pieces of paraphernalia, either original or hastily put together for the occasion. The crowd seemed impressed in any event, craning close and chattering excitedly until Julian raised his hand for silence and spoke up.

'Ladies, gentlemen, a moment of your attention, if I may. Here you see a reproduction of the first ritual used by John Aylsham in his attempts to summon the Devil. There was no reserve in his technique, and I intend to use none in my description. He would have stood as I do now, with his housemaid, Flora Martins, laid out as my assistant is now, save that Flora would have been naked, a detail we felt it best to leave out for the sake of Chloe's modesty.'

Somebody in the audience giggled and I found myself starting to blush again but Julian carried on without comment.

'There would have been others here too, most importantly Sir John's coachman and accomplice, Reuben Secker, whose body was supposed to receive the spirit of the Devil, along with a compliment of girls from the village, all doubtless well bribed, and all stark naked. Again I must apologise for failing to supply these details, but one I do intend to reproduce is the exact set of occult symbols Flora Martins had inscribed on her body. This was done with an aromatic black wax, similar to that with which the candles were made, and the symbols drawn on her body as Sir John led his acolytes in a chant.'

As he spoke he had lifted the little brass bowl of wax, to dip his finger in and begin to trace out the familiar symbols on my body. The wax felt cold and slimy, so that it was an effort to stay still as he marked first my forehead and then my cheeks, at which point a worried voice sounded from among the watching crowd.

'Don't you think it unwise to repeat the ritual so exactly? Imagine if it worked!'

Julian smiled.

'It won't. We know this because it didn't work for John Aylsham. Nor did any of the subsequent ones, or at least, so we are led to believe. Personally, I think he succeeded, and that on the night of the final ritual, Sir John Aylsham successfully summoned the Devil into the body of one of his servants, an act which cost him his life.'

A murmur ran through the crowd and I saw the edge of Julian's mouth twitch up into a brief smile before he continued.

'The facts, I think, speak for themselves. Each ritual was more elaborate than the last, and in his diaries he records increasingly curious and inexplicable phenomena, most importantly the sensation of being touched, which was apparent to both himself and to Reuben Secker, who must have been a very brave man indeed, and very loyal. We know that Sir John felt he was nearing success, and although his death means that the details of the final ritual were never recorded, subsequent events suggest that something terrible happened that night. Sir John died, for one thing, while Reuben Secker never spoke again and spent what remained of his days in a charitable foundation. Flora's hair turned white in that single night and she could never be persuaded to describe what happened, any more than could the other women who were present.'

He was making it up, but his voice was firm and even, never hesitant and absolutely serious. The audience hung

145

on every word, even those who were merely there for a day trip fascinated by what he was saying, while some of the paranormal investigators looked terrified. As he spoke he had continued to paint the symbols onto my body, neglecting only those that usually decorated my breasts and sex, and he paused to dip his finger into the pot of wax once more before he went on.

'You may say that we have no proof, and you would be right, but something happened that night and, to my mind, the weight of evidence is too heavy to allow for any mundane explanation. For one thing, it was shortly after Sir John's death that Black Shuck was first seen in the area, an apparition always associated with the Devil, while the unfortunate John Aickman had allowed Sir John's body to be reinterred in holy ground just days before his death. Then we have the tales of Black Rob Martins, Flora's son, born nine months to the day after the final ritual. His career was colourful to say the least and included smuggling, wrecking and highway robbery. He was notoriously callous, and not surprisingly ended his career on the gallows, but in the morning his body was gone. Coincidence? Perhaps, or perhaps he was the Devil's child.'

He broke off, to look around the audience with a sudden fierce stare. Several stepped backwards and I saw one woman cross herself before Julian spoke again, his voice suddenly calm and matter-of-fact.

'But I'm afraid we must move on, ladies and gentlemen, in order to make way for the next group. I do hope you've enjoyed the tour, and do feel free to explore the grounds and those parts of the house open to the public for as long as you please.'

They allowed themselves to be herded away like so many sheep, but not one failed to cast a glance back at the folly. I lay where I was, doing my best to ignore the prickling sensation that covered my skin and to push away the disturbing thoughts his speech had provoked. When the last of the visitors was gone I spoke up.

'Was any of that true?'

Julian laughed.

'Not a great deal, no, except for one or two of the names, which I borrowed from John Aylsham's diaries and the stones in the graveyard. I'd be prepared to bet that every word of it can be found on the net within a week though, even if the Inquisitor doesn't get to hear about it. Hush, and try and look as if you're expecting to be shagged by the Devil.'

'I am, later.'

It took him an instant to realise that I meant him and he smiled before turning to greet the next group from the tour, who Vanessa was leading towards us. She was as beautifully dressed as ever, and playing her part as the aristocratic hostess to perfection, but I could tell from her face that she was feeling stressed and couldn't help but wonder if it would be me or Henry she took it out on once we were alone.

Julian took over the group and went into his routine once more, as polished as ever. I did my best to relax, ignoring the rough stone beneath my body and wondering how Flora Martins would have felt in the same position, if that was indeed the name of the girl John Aylsham had used for his ritual. She would have believed in what was going on, presumably, so would either have been very frightened or have been a very wicked girl by the standards of her day. I preferred to believe the latter and, judging from some of the questions Julian was taking, our visitors were more than a little in awe of her, which made me feel better about the role I was playing and my exposure.

The second group came and went, as did the third, and the fourth, by which time the whole thing had settled down into a predictable routine. I was beginning to get bored, and stiff, using the brief gaps when we were alone to go through a few stretching exercises. Even Julian was beginning to get a little fed up, especially as each group would ask more or less the same questions, and his answers were getting shorter and less elaborate.

Finally it was done, and with the last of the tourists coaxed gently but firmly off the estate Henry brought out a tray of glasses and a bottle of cold white wine. I drank eagerly, the cool, sharp liquid quickly refreshing my senses and lifting my spirits in anticipation of what was to come. We were largely ready, with the shadows of the big trees beginning to lengthen on the bank, and when Julian went back to the house to get ready I was left with Henry. I wasn't sure what to say, as it's a little awkward when the last time you saw somebody socially they were sucking your boyfriend's penis, so I offered him a glass of wine. He hung his head before he answered in a servile tone.

'No, thank you, Miss Chloe. This evening I may only drink my mistress's wine.'

I wasn't sure what he meant, but he was obviously already in role for the evening, which made normal conversation impossible. My own role was only marginally less undignified, if at all, but I knew what he liked and ordered him to kneel. He went down immediately, onto his knees beside the altar, his eyes to the ground. I took another swallow of wine and pulled my knees up, pretending to study my toes as I scanned the reed beds in the hope of catching a glimpse of the Inquisitor. I could see the upper works of boats on the main channel and a couple of rods which presumably belonged to innocent fishermen, but nothing to suggest we were being watched. Yet the shadows under the fringes of willow and scrub oak were dense and black, making it all too easy to imagine lenses and eyes peering out from among them. I was glad when Julian returned, now wearing a long black cape.

The cape moved as he walked and I realised he was naked underneath, providing an immediate thrill of desire. I

148

hugged him as he reached the altar, then allowed one hand to slip beneath his cape, searching for his cock. He felt heavy in my hand and began to grow immediately as I pulled at his shaft with our mouths open together in a long, hard kiss. It felt nice and he made no effort to pull away, so I continued to tug on his rapidly growing hard-on. Before long his hands had gone to my breasts, first to touch, then to tug up my bikini top and spill them out, naked in the warm evening light. I thought he'd fuck me there and then, but he contented himself with stripping off my bikini top, then pulling away, now with an impressive erection thrusting up from between the sides of his cape. He glanced down, gave a satisfied nod for the state he was in, and turned me a wicked grin before he finally spoke.

'That looks the part, I think, and you'll certainly be getting the Inquisitor hot under the collar. You can get those pants off too, and make sure to give him a bit of a show, but not too obvious.'

My sense of embarrassment flared up on the instant, but I complied, rising to a kneeling position before slipping my bikini bottoms down and then turning to sit down on the altar top as I peeled them off my legs. Henry was close by, still kneeling respectfully on the ground, and I jokingly draped my discarded bikini over his head. He mumbled his thanks, then hung his head lower still as Vanessa's voice rang out from the direction of the path.

'That's what I like to see. Julian already at attention, his tart in the nude and the worm where he belongs. Right, let's get on with it.'

For all her casual attitude she looked spectacular to say the least and she obviously knew it. Her tall, slender body was enclosed in a cat suit of scarlet rubber, so tight it might have been a second skin. Knee-length black boots with spike heels lifted her to the same height as Julian, or rather more if you included the high ponytail into which she'd fixed her hair. Black leather gloves matched her boots and

149

she carried a long, thin riding crop with a wicked-looking leather sting.

Just to look at her made me want to grovel at her feet, and if the whip frightened me it also thrilled me, but not nearly as much as what she was wearing around her hips, a harness of black leather straps from the front of which protruded a dildo that put Julian's cock to shame. It was black rubber, as thick as my wrist and maybe a foot long, with a pair of monstrous balls hanging beneath. I knew where it was supposed to go, but I couldn't imagine it would fit. My fear must have showed on my face, because she laughed as she reached the altar.

'What's the matter, darling, scared you'll split? I doubt it, not the way you juice up over Julian's cock.'

My blush grew hotter still at her crude words, but it was true, the stone beneath me already wet from my excitement, and yet the dildo simply wasn't human in its proportions and I had to say something.

'Gently, please, Vanessa.'

Her answer was a snort of contempt and Julian took over.

'You'll cope, I'm sure, Chloe. Let us proceed then, and remember, we're almost certainly being watched, so make a good show of it.'

I nodded and lay back on the altar, trembling for the thought of having to accommodate Vanessa's huge dildo and no doubt Julian as well, but I did want it, badly. With my arms and legs stretched out into the points of the pentagram I was open to her, and that was all I could think about as Julian began the ritual, at least until the first drops of hot wax touched my skin from the candle he'd lifted above me. They stung – a hot pain that made me shiver and jerk for all that we'd tested the candles carefully and knew that they wouldn't burn. It was more than simple physical pain anyway, with both Julian and Vanessa smiling down on me as the hot drops splashed on my naked skin, he cool

150

and in command, she bright eyed with cruelty.

He did it all, every single one of the symbols on my body traced out in drops of wax, until my trembling had grown hard and my breathing deep and strong. My nipples were little aching cones beneath their caps of wax, my belly tight with apprehension, my sex open and wet, ready for Julian's cock. He'd been nursing his erection as he used the wax on me, keeping himself stiff and ready, and as he reached the top of the altar once more he cocked one leg up, took me firmly by the hair and slid himself into my mouth.

I sucked eagerly, allowing my thighs to come up and open in instinctive response to the big cock in my mouth, but he had quickly pulled back, his erection now glistening wet in the evening light as he once more began to chant. He hadn't mentioned the reversed sacrament to the tourists, deliberately in order to feed the Inquisitor's suspicions, but as Vanessa knelt to take his cock into her mouth I realised that he had begun it now, using his erect penis as a substitute for sacred bread.

For all her dominant poise, Vanessa sucked as eagerly as I had, as did Henry, despite the intense humiliation on his face as he accepted another man's prick into his mouth. I watched both suck, by turns jealous and excited, but more than anything proud of the way that everybody automatically accepted my man's virility. He came back to me too, slipping his cock into my mouth once more as Vanessa picked up one of the empty wineglasses from the tray.

I watched, kissing and licking at the head of Julian's cock as she lifted one elegant leg to reveal a slit in the crotch of her cat suit, with the shaved pink lips of her sex pouting beneath the balls of her strap-on. She put the glass to her pussy, her smile growing more wicked still as her muscles tensed, and then she had let go. I watched as the yellow pee swirled in the glass, quickly filling it and

151

running from the rim to splash on the ground beneath her.

She was looking down as she did it, her smile growing ever more wicked, and as she lifted the glass and held it out to me her eyes were glittering with cruel pleasure. I came off Julian's cock and took the glass, scarcely knowing what I was doing as my eyes met hers and I moved the glass to my lips. Her musky scent caught my nose and I could feel the warmth of her body through the glass, then on my lips as I sipped. My mouth filled with her taste and, after a moment of disgust, I sipped again, deliberately showing off to her and to Julian as I filled my mouth and swallowed. She nodded.

'Good girl. I knew you'd be obedient. Once more.'

I obeyed, my eyes still holding hers as I took another swallow of her pee, deliberately committing an act of submission perhaps deeper than anything I'd done before, to willingly drink the gift of my mistress's body. She knew how I felt and laughed to see the condition she'd reduced me to as she took back the glass to pass it down to Henry. He didn't hesitate at all, his face set in bliss as he swallowed down what was left in the glass in two quick gulps, then once more hung his head as he mumbled his thanks.

Vanessa ignored him, watching with her contemptuous little smile as I turned my attention back to Julian's cock, taking him as deep as I could while I stroked at the velvety skin of his balls. He'd begun to push into my mouth and, for one moment, I thought he was going to add his load to what I'd already swallowed down from Vanessa, but he pulled back at what must have been the last possible moment, to leave his cock rearing hard and wet from the front of his cape once more. I lay back into the pentagram, now in a state of submissive bliss so strong that had the ritual been real and the Devil appeared at that instant I'd have surrendered my body to him without resistance.

Julian had begun to chant in Latin, one of the rotes I

recognised from John Aylsham's diaries, a piece of liturgy spoken backwards, again and again, faster and faster, to rise to a shouted climax. I'd closed my eyes, expecting to be taken at any instant, with Vanessa's monstrous dildo thrust deep into my body as I lay spread and helpless below her. Her leg touched my open thigh as she mounted the altar, kneeling over me with the fat rubber cock pointed at my open sex as I arched my back in readiness.

'And now little Chloe ...'

Her voice broke to a yelp of astonishment at the same moment her body was slammed down onto mine. I screamed as several inches of thick rubber cock was jammed up inside me, but no louder than Vanessa, and as my eyes sprang open I saw why. Henry was on top of her, from behind, mounted on her body with his face set in demented glee as he rammed his cock in and out of her from behind. Her face was a picture, working in horrified surprise, shock and pain, and when she spoke her words were harsh and grating, addressed to Julian.

'He's up my bottom, Julian! Stop ... no, don't ... oh hell!'

She broke off with a grunt and suddenly her face had gone slack and she was sobbing out her ecstasy as her husband buggered her as if he was truly possessed. Every thrust of his cock into her anus was making the dildo jam into me, so that I was no better than her, the two of us clinging together as she was buggered. I closed my eyes to shut out the terrifying view of Henry's face, which was twisted with a savage lust I'd never have thought him capable of, but the image stayed in my mind.

Even Julian was nonplussed, but only for a moment before he'd climbed up onto the altar to straddle my head, lowering his balls onto my face as he offered his cock to Vanessa's mouth. She took him in immediately, her chin pressing to mine as she sucked him deep while I mouthed on his balls and licked at his anus. I was lost, helpless beneath them, my pussy full of thick, firm rubber, the skin of my belly and breasts slick against Vanessa's, my mouth full of my lover's balls.

Vanessa gave a sudden, choking gasp on her mouthful of cock, Henry screamed, although it was not his voice, and I realised he'd come up her bottom. But it didn't stop him, his cock still pumping hard into her to set her gagging on Julian's cock as she struggled to cope with what was being done to her. Then Julian had come too, filling her mouth and mine, and at that my own orgasm kicked in, my muscles locking hard around the huge dildo in my sex, my body jerking to the thrusts and my fingers clutching at the rough stone of the altar as I was driven to peak after helpless peak until at last I could take it no more and my senses slipped away to oblivion.

I awoke to the hot sting of whisky against my lips. Julian was bending over me, looking concerned. He pressed the whisky glass to my lips once more and I took another swallow. It burnt as it went down, making me cough, but I managed a smile and a nod when he asked if I was OK. I'd thought I was still on the altar at first, but as my head began to clear I realised that the hard surface under my back was the kitchen table in the Hall. Outside it was dark and I realised I must have been unconscious for a while. Sudden fear gripped me as I remembered Henry's face and the way he had mounted Vanessa and buggered her without a word of warning, but as my body jerked in an effort to sit up Julian took hold and laid my back onto the table, soothing me.

'It's OK, Chloe. You're fine. It just got a bit much for you, that's all.'

'But what happened? Henry ...'

'Ssh. Don't worry about it.'

'But he was ... well, it was like he was possessed!'

He laughed. 'It was, wasn't it? He says he doesn't

remember anything about it at all, but I think he saw an opportunity to get his own back for all those years grovelling at Vanessa's feet.'

'But that's what he likes, isn't it? And did you see his face?!'

'Yes, but that doesn't mean he wouldn't turn the tables if he got the chance, and he looked to me like a man who's finally got his cock up his mistress's bottom after years of being used as a servant. Besides, she's taking it out on him right now. Listen.'

He stopped talking, at which I made out a faint smack, as if of leather on flesh, then a cry of pain. Julian carried on.

'She's got him upstairs, for 100 strokes of my thick belt, and that's just for starters.'

'But she enjoyed it. You saw what she was like, and look at the way she sucked you!'

'That's the whole problem. If she'd hated it and pushed him off she wouldn't be nearly as cross, but as it is he's hurt her pride. She's going to be taking it out on him for months, which means plenty of attention and that's what he craves. She hasn't the patience or the restraint to just ignore him, which would be the only effective punishment.'

I answered with a nod, because my mind had moved on, to the way Julian had used her and me at the same time, with his balls in my mouth and his cock in Vanessa's. He hadn't even bothered to ask and I knew I should have felt cheated, but after what had happened it seemed impossibly petty to protest. It had been the four of us, after all, in a tangle of bodies over which I for one had had no control whatsoever, nor Vanessa. Yet I'd gone with my instincts and I knew that if Henry had taken me instead of Vanessa I'd have welcomed him inside me, or any other man, while Julian would have been accepted whatever happened with his usual cool, cynical style.

'We'd better get you up to bed.'

155

'No. I'm fine. I just need something to eat, and a coffee maybe.'

He shrugged, accepting my choice without further discussion, and went to the fridge. The smacks of Vanessa beating Henry and his answering cries were growing louder, but neither of us took any notice, both accepting the situation as it was. I was still naked and covered in wax, but that too seemed normal and I didn't bother to cover myself up as I sat down to the plate of cold chicken and salad Julian had set before me. He'd retrieved the wine bottle too, and poured what was left into two glasses.

We ate and drank in silence for a while, the only sound the faint, rhythmic smacks and cries coming from upstairs. Vanessa was certainly taking it out on Henry, and as I remembered the way the expression of outrage on her face had given way to ecstasy I found myself smiling, and also wondering if the moment had been captured on camera.

'Was there any sign of the Inquisitor?'

'Didn't you see the flash go off?'

'No.'

'I don't suppose you would have done, from your position. He was on a boat, I imagine, or maybe across the channel. I pretended not to notice, so hopefully he's got some good pictures.'

I made a face, reflecting that being fucked by Vanessa while sucking on my lover's balls wasn't really all that much worse than being spanked and buggered, if at all. Any remote chance I'd had of retaining my dignity was long gone, so all I could do was make the best of it. I wanted to see in any case.

'I don't suppose he'll have posted anything yet?'

'Not for a few hours, I don't suppose. We'll go up to look at his blog after dinner.'

There was nothing new, at first, and we came back down to watch Vanessa and Henry, who were in one of the formal bedrooms. He was tied up, his hands lashed behind his back, his ankles securely fixed to the feet of the huge wooden bed he was bent over, naked. She was behind him, still in her scarlet body suit, her anger and shame clear in her face as she applied Julian's belt to her husband's buttocks. I was sure he'd already had more than a hundred, and his skin was covered in thick red welts, but she seemed in no mood to stop and he wasn't protesting. When she saw us she gave me what was probably supposed to be a hard look and then quickly turned away to apply the belt to Henry's bottom with yet greater fury. I could see that she was embarrassed and moved on, resisting the temptation to gloat both out of kindness and because it seemed all too likely that she'd want to get me in the same humiliating position as Henry was, and to dish out the same painful punishment.

I washed and pulled my bathrobe on, then rejoined Julian in his room. He was grinning at the screen and I knew immediately that something had been posted. Sure enough, the Inquisitor was back and seemed to be in a state near to hysterics.

"Julian d'Alveda is the Devil. I have long suspected this, but now I know it for sure, for this very evening he summoned a satanic spirit into one of three victims coerced into his diabolic rituals. The others were the girl, Chloe, a man I didn't recognise but who had clearly been chosen to receive the evil spirit with an utter disregard for his life, and a professional dominatrix, who I suspect must have been tricked into becoming involved with promises of being paid for her professional services only to find herself penetrated anally across the altar by a man possessed!"

Julian had pulled me down onto his lap and he kissed me as he scrolled down.

'And look at this.'

It was a picture, clearly taken from the direction of the channel and showing me stripping off my bikini bottoms as Vanessa entered the temple. Others followed, photograph after photograph, some imperfectly focused, others at odd angles, but all quite clear enough to leave no doubt at all as to the details of our ritual. The last was the most shocking of all, showing the climax of our orgy, with come running from Vanessa's mouth and into mine, while Henry was crouched on her back like some demented satyr, his face frozen in a terrible leer as he pumped himself between the cheeks of his wife's bottom. My own features were mercifully obscured by Julian's thighs, although I was easily recognisable in some of the others and it was quite obvious that I'd been fucked and had my mouth used. Yet my exposure was less worrying than the way the Inquisitor was writing.

'Do you think he's dangerous?'

'Dangerous? I think he's terrified. Read on.'

I did.

"And there it is, my friends, a satanic ritual not only totally sacrilegious but successful. They didn't see me, but they have before and these people are not normal, especially Julian d'Alveda. Because of this I'm going to post here every evening, regularly. If I don't, then you know something has happened to me. Meanwhile, please spread the word as well as you are able. If you don't hear from me tomorrow night, it means that I have fallen victim to them. Goodbye, my friends."

Julian was laughing.

'He has quite an imagination, doesn't he?'

'Aren't you worried he'll call the police?'

'No. It would be good if he did, in a way, because that would give us even more publicity, and we haven't actually broken the law, so we're quite safe. He won't though, because I know his type. He's a narcissist. They always want all the attention on themselves, so if he tells the police it's out of his hands.'

'Are you sure?'

'I should know. I'm a narcissist myself. Look here.'

He had refreshed the page and I saw that the comments had started to come in. Some were sceptical, others were purely salacious, a few were against him, including one from the man who called himself Triplesix, but the majority were in support, concerned for him and outraged by our behaviour. Julian loved it, pointing out the more incensed remarks as he kneaded my bottom in his delight and excitement. I couldn't help but find his enthusiasm infectious, despite my embarrassment at some of the names I was being called, but several were saying they intended to visit the Hall, which was worrying. Julian didn't care.

'So long as they pay, that's fine. I'll tell Graham to insist that the only way to get in is to buy a ticket. He's good at that sort of thing.'

I made a face, not at all sure I wanted to face down a crowd of angry Christians, moralists and plain old-fashioned prudes, but there was no denying that we'd achieved our aim. We were going to have more interest than we could possibly cope with. Julian was thinking the same.

'We're going to have to take on new tour guides, maybe other staff as well, or rearrange things so that there's less work. You and I are definitely due for a pay rise, along with some sort of bonus scheme according to how many people we bring in.'

'We'll see about that.'

Vanessa had spoken from directly behind me and I jumped around with a guilty start, hoping Julian would defend me if she demanded that I take a beating. Julian responded casually.

'It seems fair to me, and you must admit that my idea has generated a lot of extra publicity.'

'Like I said, we'll see about that, but there's one thing I want to make absolutely clear. I am not going to be involved in any more of your rituals.'

'That's a shame. You were very good. So was Henry.'

'Don't push your luck, Julian.'

'Naturally not, and speaking of Henry, what have you done with him?'

'He's back at the gatehouse, cleaning the lavatory.'

Julian gave a complacent nod and scrolled the page up, pausing briefly to allow Vanessa to see the final picture in the Inquisitor's set, in which there was no mistaking the bliss on her face as she sucked on his cock, nor the mess dribbling down her chin, nor what Henry was doing to her. She gave a sharp, angry tut but said nothing, instead leaning forward to read the blog when the first piece of writing came on show.

'He's mad. Why would he think there's anything supernatural about what we're doing?'

'Because that's what he wants to believe, but he doesn't really make sense, does he? I mean, if I'm the Devil, why would I need to summon my spirit into somebody else's body?'

Julian was as calm as ever, and if Vanessa was flustered it seemed to be purely because of what Henry had done to her and what she'd done to him in return, but I couldn't get the image of his face out of my mind or stop myself wondering if the Inquisitor was as misguided as they thought.

Chapter Fourteen

OVER THE NEXT COUPLE of weeks I had very little time to think about him, or anything except work. Julian's plan had worked far better than we'd expected, bringing in a flood of visitors. Soon we were taking as many as we could handle, while coping with the bookings and enquiries was a full-time job in itself. We had to take on somebody to help Graham and two new guides, so that I found myself in the unfamiliar position of being in charge of other people. There was Sally, a secretary from Norwich, David, a thin young man who ran a ghost-hunting website and knew his stuff, and Carl, a Danish boy who was on a year break before university and had run out of money. All three were perfectly pleasant, but they lived on the servants' corridor in the Hall, which meant I could no longer wander around with little or nothing on or be spanked in my room.

Our evenings also changed. There were no more casual suppers over a bottle of cold white wine and followed by hot sex. The five of us ate together, taking turns to cook, which was all very cheerful and friendly but lacked the intimacy I'd come to enjoy, while after a long day's work even Julian was sometimes too tired for sex. Even when he wasn't it was more conventional, very loving and intimate, but with none of the wild, illicit thrill of being taken from behind on the moonlit lawn or spanked and then buggered out among the reed beds.

Vanessa was delighted. You could almost see the pound signs glittering in her eyes as she looked at Graham's figures or he explained how he was keeping our tax to a minimum. She'd been reluctant to give us a bonus, but had backed down after a long and heated conversation with Julian that ended in victory but also with her taking her feelings out on my bottom. That left me with more than twice as much coming in as before, and I knew I should have been happy and grateful, but instead I found myself missing the way things had been before. Candle Street Hall was beginning to lose its magic.

I didn't dare say anything, because it would have seemed ungrateful when everybody else was so pleased with themselves, except Henry. He should have been happiest of all, as what we were doing was bringing in enough money to ensure that he could keep up the home his ancestors had lived in for so many generations, but although he was full of praise for Vanessa and for Julian he obviously wasn't enjoying himself. I seldom saw him at all, as he would rise early and go out to the margins of the estate or the fens beyond, to fish or watch birds, usually staying away until the last of the tourists had left.

Ironically, the Inquisitor had also become a victim of his own success. Everybody has an equal voice on the internet, and his was soon drowned out among dozens of others discussing the Hall. To read their blogs and the forums you would have thought every single one was not only an expert on the occult but had made a lifetime's study of the Hall. The Inquisitor responded with fresh posts and more of the pictures he'd taken, keeping my sense of embarrassment on a high but failing to keep himself at the centre of attention.

Others had copied the pictures and posted them in turn, some even claiming to have taken them. The Inquisitor became increasingly shrill, the tone of his posts ever more hysterical. He added stories, completely untrue, claiming that he'd actually seen Julian grow horns and a tail, but everything he did was immediately lost in the great maelstrom of internet conspiracy theory. I'd thought he was dangerous, but now began to worry for his sanity, because in a strange way I felt he was one of us, one of the few who'd been involved before the crowds arrived.

We'd discussed the rituals and agreed that there was no point in holding any more, at least for the time being. With more visitors than we could possibly cope with and so little spare time, it seemed pointless, while for all her cool exterior Vanessa was obviously frightened by what had happened and ashamed of her own reaction. I would have liked to carry on, because I missed the thrill of it and had thoroughly enjoyed being on the receiving end of so much passion and perversity, but the best I got in the following month was a long, slow fuck from Julian with his goat's legs on so that the fur tickled my thighs as he pumped into me. It was good, but it wasn't the same.

What made us change our mind was public demand. With every tour there would be questions about when we were holding our next event at the folly, which we'd answer evasively. That alone wouldn't have been enough, but every few days somebody would take one of us aside and make a private request for inclusion in the rituals they were convinced we were holding in secret. Most were merely curious, or men who had seen my pictures and wanted to perv over me, which was both disconcerting and exciting, but there were plenty of genuine enthusiasts for the occult, even scholars from universities, and quite a few came with offers of money. These Julian recorded in a small black notebook, and late one night as we lay together on his bed in a rare moment of privacy he took it from his bedside table to show me the figures.

'Over ten thousand pounds, for a single ritual. What do you think?'

I didn't reply immediately, struggling with my morals as I considered what his suggestion entailed. They wouldn't be content with me lying on the altar in a bikini while Julian went through the motions of one of John Aylsham's rituals, of that I was sure. These were rich men, men who expected to get what they paid for, which was likely to include me in the nude – maybe to include me full stop. The thought sent a shiver down the full length of my spine and an immediate flush of shame in reaction. Julian had evidently realised the path my thoughts had taken, although perhaps not the conclusion I'd reached, and went on, his voice calm and reassuring.

'We'd have to do a full re-creation, including showing them the original diaries. Several of them have insisted on that. I imagine you'd want me to take the place of Reuben Secker, but that means we'd need a master for the ritual.'

'Who could do that? Not Henry.'

'I wouldn't think so, but one of the academics could. As for Henry, and Vanessa, I'd rather they didn't know, or any of the others.'

'They'd be sure to find out, wouldn't they?'

'Not at all. Vanessa's keen to take a break, which leaves me in charge. We give the others the evening off and we can do as we please.'

'That makes sense.'

It did, and for all my reservations about doing it, and for what he was up to, I knew I'd go along with him. After all, we'd created the demand and it was us they wanted to do the ritual, so only fair that we were the ones who benefited. More importantly, the idea was both frightening and exciting, and with Julian involved, irresistible.

Julian's idea had made life exciting once more, but that didn't mean there was any less work. The number of calls had dropped off a little, but we were still at capacity and, from the moment we opened to late in the afternoon, the Hall and grounds were always full of strangers. Vanessa had insisted that anything valuable which might have been stolen was safely locked away. Julian took her advice to heart, even removing some of the pictures and locking them in the attic, but we were still cautious of thieves, and of souvenir hunters. We were particularly careful of the library, which was kept locked at all times, so when I came across a man trying the door late one afternoon I challenged him immediately, although my instinct was to scream for Julian. He was huge, well over six feet tall, and with great brawny arms entirely covered in tattoos that included altogether too many skulls, vicious-looking beasts and grinning, impish faces. My voice had gone unusually high as I spoke up.

'Excuse me, but that area is private.'

To my surprise his voice sounded mild and educated as he replied, if very deep.

'It's the library, isn't it? I was hoping to look around.'

'It is the library, but I'm afraid it's not open to the public.'

'That's a pity, but I suppose it makes sense. You must be Chloe Anthony?'

I was used to people recognising me, in the case of men usually as they allowed their eyes to linger over the curves of my body as they remembered how I looked in the nude. He was different, perfectly frank as he extended one enormous hand. I accepted it, and although he didn't squeeze I could feel the power of his grip as he went on.

'I'm Darius King, but you might recognise me from the fora as Triplesix.'

'Um ... yes. Thanks for sticking up for us.'

'What else could I do? You've done some amazing stuff here, and you need to stand up to people like the Inquisitor. A few hundred years ago he'd have been burning witches.'

'That's rather what I thought. Do you know who he is?'

'He's called Martin Wright. He was a pagan until he got the life half frightened out of him at Clophill Church one night. Since then he's been a sort of one-man army against anything to do with alternative religion, although you couldn't really call him a Christian.'

'No? He seems to believe in the Devil. In fact he seems to think Julian *is* the Devil, but you've read his blog. Most of the latest stuff isn't true, by the way. He just seems to be after attention.'

'He's always been like that. Whatever he believes he expects everybody to follow him, even when he changes his mind. It's not going to happen, because he has all the charisma of a brick. I'd like to meet Julian, by the way, if he's about?'

'He's down at Black Dog Lane with a group of Americans. They have some apparatus which is supposed to detect paranormal emanations.'

'I don't see how that's supposed to work. If Black Shuck was there you'd see him. If he's not there, what emanations do they expect to pick up?'

'I have no idea, but they're very keen.'

'Maybe they'll get lucky.'

'Do you believe in Black Shuck?'

He gave a shrug of his massive shoulders.

'Something frightened John Aickman to death, and he's not the only one. There have been hundreds of sightings across the centuries, and nearly all run the same way. You're alone, usually at night, usually near a church. You realise you're being followed and, when you turn around, you see a great black hound. It stops when you do, but if you carry on it follows, always drawing slowly closer no matter how fast you run. Eventually it catches up with you.'

'And kills you?'

'No. There are reports of marks, but most victims die of fright. There's one tale, from Devon, not Norfolk, of a man who was walking back from the pub one night and found he was being followed by the hound. He thought it was a real dog and talked to it, even petted it, but when he reached the door of his cottage it simply disappeared. It's what you believe that matters.'

We continued to talk as we left the house and set off across the field towards Black Dog Lane. I couldn't help but feel pleased with myself, but was also slightly nervous. Darius King obviously knew a great deal more than either Julian or myself, and while he was being perfectly friendly I couldn't help but wonder how he would react if he discovered we'd set the whole thing up. Not that I could do anything about it beyond play along, and there was the satisfying moment of being able to reveal the identity of the Inquisitor to Julian. He was standing a little way apart from where a group of five middle-aged men and women were concentrating on a laptop they'd set up on a large wooden chest so I broached the subject immediately.

'Julian, meet Darius King, otherwise known as Triplesix. He knows who the Inquisitor is, a man called Martin ...'

'... Wright. He hired his boat at Chapel's in Norwich and I managed to trick the name and address out of them. I'd meant to tell you earlier but we were so crowded. Darius, hi. Julian d'Alveda. Walk down to the staithe with me.'

We walked, Julian and Darius talking politely but with increasing enthusiasm, while I couldn't help but feel a little crestfallen. Julian had produced his mobile, and as we reached the old staithe where boats had once moored to serve the village he began to tap in a number.

'I'm ringing you, Chloe. Watch this. Not me, back down the lane.'

From where we were standing at the water's edge we could see back down the lane along a tunnel of trees, gloomy even in the bright sunlight. The Americans were visible, and seemed more excited than before, pointing at the screen of their laptop and talking in urgent voices. Julian gave a soft chuckle.

'I thought that's how it worked. They're picking up

phone signals, so there's always some background activity and it gets stronger if somebody dials.'

Darius gave a bass rumble of a laugh.

'You'd think they'd realise.'

Julian shook his head.

'No. I've been with them over an hour. The guy who owns the apparatus is stringing the others along. They're on a tour, and paying quite a lot for it, I imagine, so presumably he likes to give them some results. Somebody's bound to be using a phone somewhere nearby, at least occasionally, and he simply doesn't turn the thing on until it's needed, thus guaranteeing haunting on demand.'

'You're very observant.'

'Not particularly. It had to work somehow, and as I was calling Graham when the apparatus first reacted but Black Shuck obviously wasn't coming down the lane that seemed the likely answer.'

'I was telling Chloe much the same thing. If Black Shuck's there, you can see him.'

Julian threw Darius a curious look, which changed to a grin as my phone began to ring and the voices of the Americans grew louder and more excited. I was trying not to laugh, and Darius was also amused, which eased my fears of his possible reaction to what we'd been up to. After a while Julian cut off the call and, as we turned back towards the house, Darius spoke up once more.

'I was hoping to see the library, but Chloe tells me it's out of bounds?'

'Yes, but we can have a look once everybody's gone. I'll show you John Aylsham's diaries.'

As we reached the group of Americans they all began to talk at once, bombarding Julian with questions which he fielded with his normal skill, his face grave as he admitted he'd often felt strange chills while walking down the lane. Darius and I waited a little way to one side, where the path struck out across the field toward the Hall and, after a while, he leant down to speak quietly into my ear.

'He's very good, isn't he?'

'He's brilliant.'

'But he doesn't believe, does he?'

I hesitated, then decided that Julian was likely to admit the truth anyway, which Darius had obviously already guessed.

'Er ... no.'

'He's a rationalist then? Pity. And you?'

'I'm not certain. I know most things can be explained, and like Julian says, it's stupid to assume that something supernatural is happening just because you don't understand it yourself.'

'So you're a sceptic?'

'I suppose you could say that.'

'And when you held the ritual the Inquisitor photographed, didn't you feel that was out of the ordinary?'

I was blushing immediately and couldn't think of what to say, but he didn't seem to expect an answer, starting back towards the Hall as Julian finally managed to detach himself from the Americans. Most of the day's visitors had left, and we found ourselves alone in the Hall, allowing Julian to unlock the library. It felt strangely quiet inside, once the door was fastened again behind us, and I was immediately conscious of the sense of dread, which was difficult to cope with despite knowing what it was. Darius had already told me that he knew all about it and both he and Julian ignored the sensation, talking together as we began to study the diaries.

'The ritual we performed was a simple version of the original. You know John Aylsham died during the final ritual?'

'Yes, but what changes did you make?'

'There were only four of us for a start, and he's insistent

169

that 7, 11 or 13 are the best numbers. We had a woman as the focus for the summoning as well, which isn't supposed to work.'

'And it didn't, did it? It was the other man who became possessed, wasn't it?'

'Ah, Henry, yes. That's all a bit complicated.'

'Did you arrange it so the Inquisitor would see?'

'No. It wasn't planned like that at all. Vanessa was supposed to take Chloe, and she did, only none of us expected Henry to take her in turn.'

Darius responded with a nod and Julian went back to the diary, pointing out the symbols he'd used.

'These we did exactly as he suggests. I even used the same wax ...'

He carried on, both of them discussing the ritual and use of my body in a casual manner I'd have found far from flattering except that I was very much part of the conversation. They both seemed very detached, fascinated by the technical aspects of the ritual but indifferent to the intense emotions we'd experienced and the implications of what might be to come, because it was obvious that Darius would be a useful person to have with us the next time we did it. He might even fill the role of John Aylsham himself, which meant I'd have to suck his cock, a thought at once shameful and enticing.

In the end it was me who took charge, who led them both upstairs by their hands, to one of the show bedrooms. I locked us in and kissed each of them before asking them to sit down on the bed and getting down on my knees in front of them. Neither objected, all three of us lost in the moment as I eased down first Julian's zip and then Darius's, to pull out their cocks and balls. Both were big, heavy, as men should be, and reacted quickly to the touch of my fingers and of my lips. I stayed kneeling, which felt right, sharing my favours evenly between the two of them as I teased their beautiful cocks to full erection.

As I sucked and licked, stroked and tickled, I was thinking of all the things I'd done since arriving at Candle Street Hall, of how I'd surrendered myself so completely to Julian, even my virgin anus, of how I'd allowed Vanessa to deliberately spank and humiliate me and enjoyed every moment of it, of how much pleasure I'd taken in seeing Henry given the same treatment. All of it was good, and if that made me a thoroughly wicked woman, a slut or whatever they liked to call me, then that was how I wanted it to be. Otherwise I would never have been able to kneel to two fine young men, enjoying their straining balls and erect cocks until, one after another, they had come in my mouth and I'd swallowed down all that they had to give me.

By then I needed my own climax and immediately rocked back on my heels, my thighs wide as I pulled up my dress. Both watched, understanding my need as I tugged down my knickers and began to masturbate in front of them, utterly shameless with my legs wide and my fingers working in the wetness of my sex. They'd left their cocks out, a glorious display of their virility that helped me focus on how I'd sucked them both to orgasm and that even as I rubbed myself towards ecstasy my belly was full of their come. That thought took me over the edge, and as I knelt there gasping out my passion I knew that Julian and I had found the man to be our master.

The prospect of a secret ritual involving both Julian and Darius was enough to keep me in a state of constant, mild excitement despite all the work. I still did my best to concentrate on the day-to-day running of the Hall and the business, but next to what we were up to behind the scenes it had become mundane, even tedious. Besides that, the sheer number of people involved made it impossible to provide the amount of personal attention many of the guests seemed to expect. A few even seemed disappointed that we were unable to provide ghosts to order, including one couple who told us in no uncertain terms that, at the very least, we should have built a mock-up of Lady Howard's coach of bones to drive them around the estate. Julian managed to placate them by saying what an excellent idea it was and he wished he'd thought of it himself, but they weren't the only ones and so I wasn't altogether surprised to get a call from Graham to say that there had been a complaint and that Vanessa wanted to see me.

Nothing out of the ordinary had happened over the previous few days, and as I walked down to the gatehouse I was trying to work out whom it could have been. I'd known people to be very quiet and then complain that they hadn't had enough attention, but everybody in my groups had seemed perfectly happy, so I was genuinely puzzled as I climbed the stairs to the Aylsham's flat. Vanessa was on the sofa, even more smartly dressed than usual, in a dark grey skirt suit with a red stripe, a silk blouse, seamed stockings and polished black heels. As always she made me feel scruffy, and small, all the more so when she addressed me.

'When are you going to smarten yourself up, Chloe?'

'I'm sorry, Vanessa, but ...'

'It's Lady Aylsham today, and I don't really expect you to answer my question as I realise that you're a hopeless sloven. Now ...'

She trailed off as she reached for a piece of paper. I knew she was playing with me, or at least, half playing, as if it had been anything serious she wouldn't have insisted on being called Lady Aylsham. That probably meant I was going to get a spanking, which I wasn't really in the mood for, but I told myself I'd be all right once my bottom was warm. I knew better than to protest and stayed quiet until she'd finished reading what was on the sheet of paper and spoke up again.

'A Mr and Mrs Anstruther say that you were extremely

172

rude to them, that you wouldn't answer their questions and that you told them to be quiet. Well?'

'Mr and Mrs Anstruther? I don't even remember them.'

'That's rather the problem, isn't it, Chloe? You need to pay more attention to individual visitors. So, what's to be done with you, do you suppose?'

I hung my head in genuine chagrin, knowing that whatever I said the outcome would be the same: a trip over her knee with my knickers pulled down, unless I refused point blank, but I already half wanted it and she knew exactly how to get to me. It seemed pointless to delay the inevitable, but if I was having trouble raising my eyes from the carpet and my voice was a mumble as I answered her, there was nothing fake about my reaction.

'I suppose I ought to be spanked, Lady Aylsham.'

Her mouth flickered into a cruel smile, but only for a moment before she went on.

'So you think you ought to be spanked, do you? How many times have I had to spank you since you arrived here, Chloe?'

'I ... I don't know, Lady Aylsham.'

'You've lost count, haven't you? That's no surprise, and as a matter of fact, so have I, which just goes to show that it's not having much effect, is it?'

'No, Lady Aylsham, I suppose not.'

'No effect at all, and we both know why, don't we?'

I wasn't sure what the answer was supposed to be, when it was all a game anyway, but I took a guess.

'Because I enjoy it too much?'

She gave a snort of contempt.

'You're a slut, Chloe Anthony. What are you?'

'A slut, Lady Aylsham.'

'Yes, you're a slut, and yes, it's because you enjoy it too much. A punishment is meant to hurt, Chloe.'

'It does hurt!'

'Not enough, which is why I'm going to cane you,

173

Chloe.'

I must have made a silly face as I remembered the sting of her riding whip, because she laughed, only for her expression to suddenly become serious as she carried on.

'I mean what I say, Chloe. This is intended to hurt, and to make you pay a bit more attention to the job I'm paying you for, and paying you well, I might add.'

She sounded genuinely cross, and I was a bit taken aback by the vehemence of her words, which left me wondering to what extent she was playing and to what extent the punishment was intended to be real. I began to answer, wanting reassurance that she wouldn't be too harsh with me, but before I could speak she had lifted something from behind the sofa, something that shut me up – an old-fashioned school cane with a crooked handle, long and brown and as thick as a finger. She nodded as she read the fear in my eyes.

'That's right, Chloe, this is what I'm going to use on that fat little bottom of yours, hard. Now get those jeans and panties down and touch your toes.'

My fingers went straight to the button of my jeans, but I was begging for mercy even as I began to prepare myself.

'Couldn't you just spank me, Van ... Lady Aylsham? Or at least spank me first so it doesn't hurt so much?'

She laughed and put the cane to one side, filling me with relief but also shame for being so pathetic. I knew I could have told her to go to hell, or played the game and taken my caning like a big girl instead of begging to have my bottom smacked first, but it was now too late. She had one finger crooked and was beckoning me forward. I went, to lie myself across her knees in that same awful position she, and Julian, had held me several times before, the position in which a girl is spanked.

My jeans were already wide open and she'd quickly pulled them down, tugged the tight blue denim over my hips and bottom to leave my knickers on show. I knew full well those would be coming down too, but she couldn't resist tormenting me with a few smacks across my panty seat to let me think I might be allowed to keep at least a little modesty. It worked too, my hope rising despite myself, only to give way to embarrassment and shame as my knickers were peeled down over my bottom. She began to spank me again, harder now, and to talk to me as she did it.

'How can you bear to let another woman do this to you, Chloe? Over my knee with your knickers pulled down for a spanking? How does it feel? How does it really feel, with your bottom bare for me to smack, and you actually get off on it?! Don't you have any self-respect at all, Chloe? Don't you have any pride, to let yourself be spanked like this? Spanked, Chloe, spanked on your bare bottom.'

She laughed, bringing me fresh shame and adding to my helpless and rapidly increasing excitement. I wanted to try and explain to her how natural it felt, and how good, maybe even to remind her how much she'd enjoyed Henry's cock up her own bottom, but I knew it would only get me into deeper trouble. She'd got to me though, badly, the tears already trickling down my cheeks as the spanking grew gradually harder, until I'd begun to kick my legs and toss my hair about in helpless reaction, with my thighs cocked wide to show off my sex behind and my cheeks spreading with every slap to expose my anus.

I thought she'd carry on, bringing me fully on heat so that I could cope with the cane as well as possible, but as soon as I'd begun to gasp and push my bottom up she stopped. My fear picked up on the instant, giving way to hope as her hand settled on my now hot bottom and she began to touch me up, only to come back once more, stronger than before, as she spoke up.

'Up you get then, you big baby. Get in position, touching your toes the way I told you, and now that you're nice and warm I think I'll make it 12 rather than six.'

175

'But Lady Aylsham ...'

'OK, 18.'

I shut up, not daring to say more, and got to my feet. My face was wet with tears, my hair a bedraggled mess, my bottom hot and red with my jeans and panties in a tangle around my ankles as I shuffled to the centre of the room. She retrieved the cane as she stood up, and I was feeling thoroughly sorry for myself as I bent over to present her with my bare bottom, painfully aware of the show I was making of the dark little hole between my cheeks and of my very wet sex but unable to bring myself not to obey.

She got behind me, her mouth twitching in cruel glee and her eyes bright with satisfaction as she laid the cane across my backside. I shut my eyes, braced myself for the pain and determined not to give her the satisfaction of hearing me scream, for all that I'd been crying since the beginning of my spanking. She pressed the cane to the flesh of my bottom, lifted it and brought it down, hard, to lay a line of searing fire full across my cheeks and set me jumping and screaming, my resolve lost immediately as the pain kicked in. I nearly tripped over my own lowered clothes, and only just managed to keep my balance, with Vanessa barking at me as I clutched at the table to stop myself going over.

'Stay still, can't you! Honestly, the fuss you make over getting your bottom whacked.'

'It hurts!'

'It's supposed to hurt, stupid. Now get that fat bottom back up. That's right, well up so I can see your cunt, and hold onto your ankles. That way perhaps you'll manage to keep still.'

I'd got back into the humiliating position she'd demanded of me, biting my lip in pain and frustration as for the second time the cane was settled across the cheeks of my bottom, lifted and brought down. Once again I screamed and jumped, completely unable to cope with the shock of impact and the fiery pain of the welt she'd planted across my flesh, but this time I'd quickly caught hold of my ankles again. Vanessa gave a soft chuckle.

'Good girl, you're learning. You see, it's much easier if you do as you're told, isn't it?'

'Yes, Lady Aylsham.'

I'd said it, but I was ashamed for my own words, and the submissive streak in me that kept me holding onto my ankles with my arse stuck in the air while some vicious bitch got her kicks by caning me. Not that I could even pretend I didn't want it, with the juice from my sex running down my thighs just as the tears were running down my face. I even told myself that I deserved it, that I needed to be beaten for being rude to the Anstruthers, although I still couldn't remember who they were. That seemed right, and as Vanessa tapped the cane across my bottom I spoke up once more.

'Thank you for my punishment, Lady Aylsham.'

'You really are learning.'

The cane bit into my flesh for the third time, and for the third time I screamed and jumped, stamping up and down in my panties and jeans for a moment before getting back in the position she wanted me, but keeping my hold on my ankles. Vanessa told me I was a good girl and I immediately felt grateful, pathetically grateful. With the fourth stroke I managed to stay down as before, and the fifth, for all that my bottom was now burning hot all over and the tears streaming from my eyes, tears of misery – and of ecstasy too. I was hers completely, spanked and caned into a state of grovelling submission, and grateful for my punishment.

As the caning continued I found myself wishing the Anstruthers were there to watch me beaten, so that I could apologise to them properly, maybe suck his cock and lick her out. I'd lost count of the cuts too, relying on Vanessa to do justice to my bottom with the full 18 strokes of the cane she'd awarded me, and which I now wanted and felt I deserved. She continued, cool and poised in her beautiful clothes as she beat me, stroke after stroke, with me stripped half bare and blubbering in my pain. At one point she pushed up my top and bra to leave my breasts naked, but when she paused again to take them in her hands I assumed she was only doing it to add to my humiliation before she carried on. When she spoke it was more to herself than to me, musing on the size and weight of my breasts as she fondled me.

'I wonder how it feels to be built like you, with a pair of great, fat, ungainly udders. Still, the boys like them, don't they?'

She gave me a slap, then took hold of one nipple and pulled hard, twisting at the same time. I cried out and she laughed, her hand tightening in my hair to pull me upright. Again she slapped my breasts, and again, full across both to make my flesh sting and leave my nipples achingly stiff.

'What a little slut you are, Chloe. Now, down on the rug, on your back.'

I knew what she was going to do to me and went down without hesitation, my hand already on my breasts as I gave in to the need to play with myself, only to receive a kick to one shoulder.

'You can cut that out, for a start. This is a punishment, Chloe, not a bit of fun. I'm going to sit on your face, and you are going to lick my bottom. Keep your hands by your side while you're doing it and don't stop until I tell you to. Got it?'

'Yes, Lady Aylsham.'

'Good.'

She'd straddled my head as she spoke, planting one immaculate high heel to either side. I could see up her skirt, to the tops of her stockings, the turn of her bottom cheeks and her pussy, quite bare. She had no knickers on, which meant she'd planned out every detail in advance, knowing I'd accept both the punishment and having her sit on my face. It was no surprise, and she'd been right, because I found myself pushing my tongue out even as she began to tug her skirt up to get her bottom bare.

As she sank down into a squat her cheeks spread, showing off the tight dimple of her anus, which I was going to lick, my tongue stuck up another woman's bottom hole to pleasure her, a woman who'd just spanked and beaten me. It was an awful thing to do to somebody, to beat them then make them lick her bottom, but she knew me all too well, her voice full of cruel delight as she spoke again.

'Just look on it as the price of being a dirty little bitch. Now get your tongue up me.'

She'd settled herself onto my face, her perfect little bottom cheeks spread well apart, her anus pressed to my mouth. I began to lick immediately, unable to stop myself and wishing only she'd let me play with my pussy and breasts so that I could share in her ecstasy. She made very sure I didn't, spreading out my arms and kneeling on them so that I was trapped. It hurt, and she had a lot of her weight settled on my face, but there was nothing I could do, my tongue now pushed well up her bottom hole as she began to masturbate.

'There we are, Chloe, how does that feel, with your fat bottom thrashed and your tongue up your mistress's arsehole? God, but it's where you belong, with your dirty angel's face as a seat for my bottom. That's it, lick, lick me, you little slut ... you filthy little slut!'

She broke off with a gasp and the motion of her fingers on her sex had suddenly grown firmer and faster, poking at my chin as I struggled to get my tongue as deep up her bottom hole as it would go. I felt her cheeks tighten in my face and I knew she was coming, and that when she'd taken her pleasure of me I would be allowed mine. Even as she cried out in ecstasy my thighs had come up and open, and as she relaxed slowly onto my body, I was struggling to get my arms out from under her legs so that I could show her what she'd done to me by deliberately bringing myself off in front of her with my tongue still up her bottom. One arm came free, then the other and I was doing it, only to be brought up short as she snatched them away.

'Oh no you don't, you dirty little bitch. Keep your hands to yourself!'

As she spoke she'd lifted her bottom a little and, after gasping in a badly needed mouthful of air, I began to beg, sure she was only teasing me.

'Please, Vanessa, please! I need to come. You know I need to come! Please let me.'

I was trying to get my hands to my pussy as I spoke, but she wouldn't let me. As she climbed off she let go, but only to slap me hard across my face.

'Stop it, I said! That was a punishment, Chloe.'

'But Vanessa, please!'

'No. I enjoy your frustration, and you need to remember that you are here to serve me. Now fuck off.'

The moment was gone, her nastiness no longer a turn-on. I stood up, feeling utterly wretched as I adjusted my clothes but still hoping she'd take pity on me. One word and I'd have been spread out on the floor, masturbating openly in front of her with all the burning shame in my head focused towards what would have been a beautiful orgasm. She ignored me completely, not even bothering to say goodbye as she made for the kitchen.

I made my way back down the stairs, feeling sorry for myself and badly in need of comfort. Julian was in Norwich, which was no doubt why Vanessa had chosen that moment to punish me, so I was going to have to wait, and I was feeling so small that as I reached the office even Sally's friendly but casual smile nearly brought the tears back to my eyes. I needed to talk, badly, just ordinary human conversation, while I also wanted to know more about the couple who'd complained about me and given

180

Vanessa the excuse she wanted to beat me. I turned to Graham.

'There were a couple in one of yesterday's groups, a Mr and Mrs Anstruther. Can you bring their details up for me?'

He looked to Sally, who typed in a search query, waited a moment, typed in another, then turned from her screen.

'No Mr and Mrs Anstruther, or anything like that.'

'Are you sure? They'd have been here in the morning I think.'

'Certain. You can check for yourself. There's nobody of that name down for yesterday, or any other time.'

Vanessa had made it all up, simply for the pleasure of making me believe my caning was a real punishment. I'd fallen for it, which left me feeling smaller still as I walked back towards the Hall. It was just too much, the final straw, and despite a few minutes of desperately trying to stop myself I was soon spread out on my bed with my boobs out and my knickers and jeans around my ankles, just as I had been for Vanessa, drowning in my own shame as I rubbed myself to orgasm over what she'd done to me.

Chapter Fifteen

I WASN'T AT ALL happy about the way Vanessa had behaved. Admittedly I'd enjoyed it, once I was over the pain, but I'd have been perfectly happy to let her punish me for fun, as she'd done before. Obviously she needed to feel that I was genuinely under her control, but as an excuse that only went so far, and I felt that at the very least she might have given me a hug before sending me away. Really she should have let me come and then given me a proper cuddle, as she knew perfectly well, which left me feeling that she took pleasure in really hurting me.

Fortunately I had the consolation of being up to no good behind her back and, from then on, what little guilt I'd felt about it vanished altogether. She could use me as a toy for her sadistic fantasies, that was fine, but only if she played fair. As she hadn't, she had no claim on my loyalty, and I threw myself into the arrangements with new zeal. I also told Julian what had happened, half hoping he'd go down to the gatehouse, haul the little bitch across his knee, pull down her expensive panties and spank her until she howled, preferably in front of a large tour party. Instead he cautioned me to be calm, and patient.

'I'll sort it out for you, Chloe, I promise, but not now. We need Vanessa on side at the moment, so that there's no difficulty with the ritual.'

I could see his point, but couldn't help but feel indignant.

'Couldn't you at least explain things to her? I do like

what she does to me, and I do like to feel mistreated, for sex, but I still need her respect, if that makes any sense.'

'It makes perfect sense, to me, probably not to Vanessa. She prefers to get her own way without any fuss, and she is a genuine sadist. My advice is to take what you can from her, just as she takes what she can from you. Believe me, *I* intend to.'

'How do you mean?'

'You'll see. For now, just trust me.'

He took my head in his hands and kissed me on the forehead as he spoke, a gesture I couldn't help but enjoy, for all that I'd have found it condescending from any lesser man. I was also curious about his plans for Vanessa, but knew better than to push him, so snuggled up to his chest instead. He gave me a squeeze then carried on.

'Never mind Vanessa anyway, because there's something I need you to do.'

'Anything.'

He laughed.

'You might want to wait until I've told you what it is before making rash promises, but it is important. A lot of our clients are worried about their pictures ending up on the net, and while I've told them they'll be able to wear cowls, that only goes so far. We need to make sure the Inquisitor isn't about.'

'I thought we'd scared him off?'

'Maybe, maybe not, but I want to be sure, and that's where you come in.'

I could see where the conversation was going and my stomach had begun to tighten, but I let him talk.

'The Inquisitor, Martin what's-his-name, comes across as a religious fanatic, and that may be true, but I think his real problem is jealousy. It's always the way with religious types who are not getting their rocks off. They can't bear to see other people having fun and use their beliefs as an excuse to try and put a stop to it, or at least to make sure

184

they get a good look at what's going on. He knows we're having a lot of fun and he's not involved, so he wants to stop us, but if he ...'

I knew what he wanted, which would be the ultimate sacrifice I could make to prove my love to him, and broke into the flow of his words.

'It's all right, Julian. I understand. You want me to let him fuck me.'

He looked around in surprise.

'Fuck you? No, nothing like that. I just need you to let him think he's got a date with you on the night we arrange the ritual.'

'Oh.'

I'd gone crimson with embarrassment, both for what I'd said and for being such a slut, but the moment he'd told me I wasn't going to have to surrender my body at his request I'd felt not relief, but disappointment. Julian merely laughed, which made my blushes hotter still, but he didn't seem to notice as he carried on talking.

'We know who he is and we know where he lives, so it should be simple. You turn up, in some suitably gothic outfit which leaves plenty of cleavage on show, tell him we want him to leave us alone, flirt a little and promise to take him to bed in return for peace and quiet. He's bound to accept, and when we decide on a date you tell him that will be the night. You'll have told him to meet you somewhere else entirely, Cromer for instance, and he'll have a frustrating evening while we complete the ritual in peace.'

'What if he wants it then and there?'

'Put him off. Surely you can think up a suitable excuse?'

'I suppose so. Sorry, I thought ... I ...'

'Hush. You're such a trollop, Chloe, but I love you for it.'

He kissed me again, this time on my nose, and I managed a smile as his hands began to explore my breasts.

The Inquisitor, Martin Wright, had a Great Yarmouth address. Discovering his name had already robbed him of some of the mystery we'd built up around him, and I had come to imagine him as a middle-aged man probably still living with his mother on one of the new estates at the fringes of the town. I knew from Darius that Wright was still in his 20s, but that had only gone so far to dispel the image and I was surprised to find myself outside a detached cottage set in a badly neglected garden a couple of miles to the north of the town, where low hills pushed up from the flat country.

Julian was parked a little way down the lane, just out of sight, easing my fear for visiting a lone man in such a secluded spot, but it still took a lot of effort to maintain my poise as I walked to the door. There was an ancient bell pull, which created a muffled clanging within the house, dying slowly until the door came open with a jerk to reveal a solidly built man with a mop of sandy hair wearing nothing but a pair of tatty tracksuit bottoms. He recognised me immediately, his eyes flickering from my face to my chest and back.

'Chloe Anthony! Where's D'Alveda?'

As he spoke he had thrust his head out from the door, looking from side to side as if expecting to find Julian half hidden behind an overgrown rose bush. I tried to reassure him.

'He's not here, Mr Wright. We need to talk.'

He ignored me, stepping out from the cottage to the front gate and glancing up and down the lane. I waited, rehearsing what Julian had told me to say in my head until he turned back once more to look me up and down with eyes full of suspicion.

'What are you doing here?'

'I want to make you an offer, Mr Wright.'

He hesitated just an instant before answering, again

allowing his gaze to flick to my breasts. I expected him to say something dramatic, like "Get thee behind me, Satan!", but he was more practical.

'What could you possibly offer that I'd want?'

We both knew the answer, he in his dirty little mind and me from the desperation in his voice. I smiled, doing my best to play my part for all that I could scarcely believe it was me speaking the words as I answered him.

'I know very well what you want, Mr Wright ... Martin. You want what you've seen. What Julian has – me.'

As I spoke I'd stepped forward, until we were just inches apart. He swallowed, shaking his head either in denial or disbelief, but his eyes were now fixed firmly on my cleavage and I pressed my advantage.

'That's what you want, isn't it, Martin? Think of what you've seen, how naughty I've been. All of that could be yours, if you'll just agree to do me a little favour in return.'

Julian had read him right, no question. I'd never had a man want me so badly, or at least, not until he was just about to come, and from the look on Martin Wright's face he might well have been. He was a lot more attractive than I'd expected as well, but that was less important than his desire for me and the power it gave me. As I pushed him inside his cottage I realised that my task was going to be easy.

The interior was a mess, with paper and bits of gadgetry strewn everywhere, so that the only clear place to sit in his living room was the huge black leather chair in front of the computer. I took it, feeling the leather still warm as I settled down, and as I put my elbow on his desk I jogged the mouse. His screen came to life, showing the background, which was a large and colourful picture of me, bent over Julian's knee as I was prepared for spanking in front of the snail man, with my panties just far enough down to show off my bottom hole and pussy. The sight nearly broke my poise, but I managed to turn my shock and embarrassment into a haughty look and did my best to imitate Vanessa's voice as I spoke to him.

'You dirty little boy.'

He was standing in the doorway, looking sorry for himself, and immediately began to stammer apologies, so I pressed my advantage.

'I don't mind. Those of us who worship the true Lord rejoice in our bodies, and in the gift of pain. And you, as you obviously like to see me spanked, perhaps you're not so very white after all?'

I was making it up as I went along, but it seemed to impress him as he was rooted to the spot, watching me with his eyes full of lust and fear. At last he managed to find his voice.

'I ... I wouldn't do that to you. I'd be nice to you. I'm a nice guy. I'd look after you. I'm quite well off.'

It wasn't the response I'd been expecting at all, and suggested he was more obsessed with me than I'd ever have guessed, but I did my best to get him back on track.

'Julian is my lover, Martin, and there is no man who can be his equal, but you know he gives me to others, don't you?'

He nodded, no doubt thinking of Vanessa and her monstrous strap-on dildo. Now he knew I was available, or he thought he did, and he'd begun to sweat. I was thoroughly enjoying my power as I went on.

'Yes, Martin, he gives me to others, and he is prepared to give me to you, so long as you promise to leave us alone at Candle Street Hall. That means no peeping, or if you must peep, then what you see stays firmly in that dirty little mind of yours, got it?'

He nodded earnestly, and really that was all I needed to do, but I couldn't bring myself to simply leave. It was all too much fun. I decided to take him to the brink before I told him he wasn't going to get anything until later, only to remember how cross I'd been with Vanessa for giving me the same treatment. I was also very sure that if I made him come he would be far more obedient than if I left him frustrated, especially if he was sure there would be more to follow at a later date. The situation was also turning me on, both for his helpless desire and because I knew how Julian would react, maybe even turning the tables on me with a good, long spanking for being such a slut. I lifted my breasts in my hands, and on sudden impulse tugged down the front of my little black dress and the cups of my bra with it, to expose myself. His eyes went round and his mouth came slowly open as I spoke to him.

'Do you like my breasts, Martin? Aren't they big, and so heavy. Julian likes to put his cock between them, and while that privilege is reserved for him, maybe I'll let you watch while I play with them and you can pull off your little prick. How would that be?'

He gave another nod, apparently unable to find words, but that was all. I began to play with my nipples, but he just stood there, gaping like a goldfish and I was forced to give him a little encouragement.

'Come along then, down with your trousers. Let's see what you've got.'

I could tell that he was erect, because his cock made a hard bar even beneath the loose material of his tracksuit trousers. He didn't look small at all and I genuinely wanted to see, but still he didn't move, merely mumbling something incoherent. I got up, walked across to him, still playing with my breasts, only to suddenly duck low and jerk his tracksuit bottoms down to reveal his erection, every bit as long and thick as I'd expected, but straining out a pair of lacy bright pink panties.

'Why, you dirty little pig!'

'I'm sorry.'

He sounded so wretched I thought he was going to cry, but despite what I'd said he'd misread my reaction. The sight of his erect cock trapped in girl's underwear was obscene, but deliciously obscene, and far from being repelled I now wanted to pop him free of the tight pink lace and straight into my mouth. I hesitated, telling myself not to be such a slut, then thought of how Julian would laugh, and what he'd do to me.

'Sit down, you filthy little pervert. I'm going to suck you off.'

I gave him a gentle push as I spoke. He went back, flopping down onto a sofa piled with magazines and newspapers. I came forward, now on my knees, my dignity forgotten in my eagerness to play with his cock. His trousers were right down, leaving him showing it all, with his big cock straining in the tiny pink panties as I moved a large dog bowl aside so that I could crawl closer, to touch, feeling how hard he was through the lace.

A heavy, shame-filled moan escaped his lips as I began to stroke his cock through the panties, and again as I did what I really wanted to, pulling them open to free his erection into my mouth. He was hot and hard, very suckable indeed, and as I lifted his balls out of his panties I knew I had to come too. I set to work, fulfilling my promise by sucking his cock for him, but playing with myself at the same time, first with my breasts so that he could watch, then with my pussy, my hand thrust deep down my tights and panties as I once more began to tease his balls.

I was fairly sure he'd been wanking before I arrived at the cottage, maybe over his pictures of me, which only made my situation more exciting. He'd seen me stripped and spanked, fucked up my pussy and fucked up my bottom, used by Julian in all sorts of delicious ways. And now, because Julian had ordered it, he had me down on my knees and sucking his cock, sucking his cock with my breasts bare, the way dirty boys like it, and he was nothing if not dirty, to dress up in girly pink knickers while he wanked over pictures of me getting a spanking.

My pleasure was already rising towards orgasm when he came, deep in my mouth with one spurt, only for me to pull back and take the second in my face on purpose. He cried out in ecstasy as I deliberately soiled myself, and again as a third spurt went into my open mouth and I was rubbing his cock in my face as my own orgasm kicked in, with little jets of come squeezing out to soil my cheeks and eyes and lips – and, at the very peak of my own ecstasy, I swallowed.

I told Julian what I'd done, in exact detail, and I got my spanking, then and there, over the bonnet of the car in the lane before he took me from behind, still with the taste of the Inquisitor's come in my mouth as my lover's filled my sex. It was a gloriously rude thing to do and the perfect finish to what had been a complete success. I had Martin's number and he'd agreed to take me out for the evening in Cromer. All that remained was to set the date for the ritual.

We chose the equinox, which Darius said was the Feast of Mabon and an ideal day, while it gave Julian time to ensure that all the interested parties would turn up and pay up. The number attending was a problem, as Darius wanted to keep it to 13 but we had 27 people interested. The amount of money they were offering also varied greatly, which might have caused problems had not Julian announced that the more they paid the more intimately they could be involved in the ritual. Darius knew nothing of this, just as Vanessa, Henry and our fellow staff knew nothing at all, creating layers of secrecy and plenty of minor difficulties, all of which Julian handled with his usual skill.

The feel of autumn was in the air long before the actual day, with cool breezes rustling the reed beds and the trees around the folly and along Black Dog Lane turning from green to gold. With the end of the school holidays the number of people visiting the Hall had dropped sharply, while the novelty of the sensation created by Julian and I on the net was also beginning to wear off. Takings were still good, and only Vanessa seemed concerned, insisting we reduce our staff but still more than happy to go off on the holiday Julian had suggested.

Julian himself was unconcerned and obviously enjoying himself, and me. With the Hall now quieter he could take me out into the grounds for sex, frequently on the altar and frequently up my bottom, while he introduced me to a regular regime of spankings and lengthy sessions of sucking his cock on my knees. When Darius visited I would take him in my mouth as well, until entertaining two men at once seemed like second nature. All of it was good for me, keeping me on a pleasant erotic high, although in occasional quiet moments I would wonder over how much I'd changed in the space of one short summer.

We also played with Vanessa, whose need to exert her dominance had grown stronger than ever since her experience with Henry. She loved to make him suck Julian's cock, and to have me lick her, either on my knees at her feet or sitting astride my head so that she could have me attend to her bottom hole as well as her sex, usually after I'd been well spanked or given a taste of the cane or belt. I coped well enough, enjoying her attentions as Julian had suggested, and on the odd occasion, when it all got a bit much, simply reminding myself of how she'd looked as Henry squeezed his cock up her bottom.

The day she and Henry left for the Maldives cranked my excitement up another notch. Now we were in charge, or more accurately, Julian was, but we could do as we pleased. Graham stayed in the background as always, while he and Sally had become an item which made things easier still. The other two were gone, enabling us to invite Darius to stay while we made the final arrangements for the ritual.

When he arrived I'd been taking a shower after the last of the day's tourists had left and I heard him talking to

Julian downstairs. I didn't bother to dress, merely wrapping a towel around myself as I padded down to the kitchen, and I'd quickly discarded that. Being naked in front of them felt not just natural, but right, how I should be and the perfect expression for my joy in exhibiting myself.

I knew I would be having sex with both of them that night, but nobody said anything. We didn't need to. Instead our conversation ranged over several topics while we drank wine together and Julian cooked. Only when we'd finished and had sat together for a while with the sinking sun striking in through the windows did I react, easing Julian's zip down to free his cock into my hand, then Darius's. It felt wonderful to have two heavy, gloriously male cocks growing in my hands as they gently stroked my body, exploring my breasts and thighs, the curve of my hips and, once I'd let my thighs part, my sex.

Neither rushed me, both content to allow me to tug his cock to full erection before I was ready for more. I went down on my knees, which was absolutely where I belonged, to use my mouth on them in turn, licking and sucking at their balls and their beautiful big erections in an act of open worship for their virility. Soon I had Julian in my mouth while I pulled at Darius, before having them rise and come together so that I could suck them, turn and turn about. I even tried to get them both in my mouth at once, but it wouldn't work, and with that they finally lost patience with me.

I was put over the kitchen table, the plates and glasses pushed to one side to make room for my body, with my bottom stuck out at one side and my mouth available at the other. Julian came behind me, to reward me with a few firm slaps across my cheeks as Darius fed his cock into my mouth, then to enter me, deep and hard, thrusting into me from behind until they'd found a rhythm. I was in heaven, rocked back and forth on their cocks, one in at each end, lost to everything but the pleasure of my fucking.

Even when they swapped around I barely noticed, waiting with my eyes closed in bliss until I was filled once more. They were more urgent now, with Darius gripping my hips as he thrust into me from behind and Julian as deep into my mouth as he could get. I'd never felt so completely full of cock, with my entire being focused on the two men who were pleasuring themselves in me. It could have gone on for ever, the way I felt, but both of them were getting faster and rougher, until I could barely take what was being done to me.

They came in unison, each pulling free at the last instant, Julian to do it in my face and Darius all over my bottom and between my cheeks. Even as the hot fluid spattered my skin my hand had gone back between my legs and I was masturbating furiously, in desperate need for my own climax for the way they'd treated me and still wanting more. They didn't disappoint, using their cocks to rub what they'd done on me into my face and over my bottom, which drove me up to a climax almost as strong as when I'd fainted on the altar, but even then I knew that what I was getting was only a foretaste of what was to come.

They took me twice more that night and again in the morning, but after that we were forced to get on with our work. I was blissfully happy, all my reservations swept away on a tide of arousal and satisfaction, happy to have done so many of the things I'd only ever fantasised about before coming to Candle Street Hall, or not even that. Julian was also on his best form, dealing with each day's visitors with practised ease before we went down to the folly and prepared the altar, which led to another bout of eager, unrestrained sex before we returned to the Hall.

Everything was now ready, with the following day cleared for our special guests, our parts carefully memorised and everything we'd need ready for use. I felt a bit of a bitch when I called Martin Wright to make a date I had no intention of keeping, but I knew it was necessary and consoled myself with the thought of the pleasure I'd given him on my visit. He accepted eagerly, allowing me to inform Julian that we were definitely safe, while we had arranged for our guests to wear cowls in any case, under which most would be naked, as would I be.

In the morning I didn't even bother to dress, but on a sudden whim shaved my pubic hair into a five-pointed star, which delighted both Julian and Darius. They were handling the guests as they arrived and there was no reason for me to go anywhere near the gatehouse, so I stayed naked all day, with my sense of anticipation gradually rising. People began to arrive early in the afternoon, academics and cultists, devoted Satanists and the merely curious, all united by their interest in John Aylsham's ritual and in what was to be done to me.

I'd never known so much attention, 21 men and six women, all focused on me, and not only that but with as much interest in me as a person as in my body. They all wanted to talk to me, and to look me over with a frank admiration I couldn't help but enjoy. Inevitably some of them took advantage of my nudity to touch, squeezing my thighs, stroking or patting my bottom, even caressing my breasts or teasing my nipples to make them stiff, but I found myself unable to resent the attention. I'd been soaking wet before any of them arrived and, by the time they were ready to go down to the folly, I could think of nothing but sex.

Julian had gone ahead, to make sure that each of them knew their role, leading a procession of cowled men and women down the path between the trees. Some wore robes, others were naked, according to their role, allowing me glimpses of cocks already half stiff with excitement for their pawing of my body. Darius was to lead me down to the folly and stayed back, stripping naked in the kitchen to reveal his massive, heavily muscled body with the tattoos coiling down his arms and legs and his huge cock and balls hanging heavy between his thighs. With his robes on he came close to where I was sitting, his voice deeper and richer than ever as he gave me an order.

'Suck me erect.'

I obeyed without hesitation, taking his penis into my mouth to roll back his foreskin with my teeth and suck on the meaty head within. He took the treatment in silence, but was soon pushing into my mouth as I sucked and licked, performing all the little tricks Julian and others had taught me to get men excited. Soon he was hard, his beautiful cock a great column of flesh, supremely virile and good enough for anybody's mouth, woman or man.

It stuck out from the sides of his robe, just as Julian's had done, and I took hold, to nurse his erection as we walked down the path to where we could see lights among the trees. The others were all in place, Julian and the chosen few within the folly, the remainder arranged around it as if at the points and junctions of a pentagram. All of them watched as Darius and I approached, their faces half concealed beneath their cowls creating an eerie impression, but I had no fear. I was one of them, and more – the object of their attention.

Darius took my hand as we reached the folly, leading me inside. Julian helped me up onto the altar and I spread myself out as before, with my head and limbs at the points of the pentagram among the skulls with their burning candles on top, each now thick with wax. Darius began to chant as he took up the pot of black wax and my muscles jerked to his touch as he began to inscribe the symbols on my body. I struggled to lie still, my breathing growing gradually deeper, my body shaking, my emotions in turmoil as I fought my rising desire. My mouth had come wide, and I couldn't stop myself from bringing up my knees to spread out my sex, wet and open, ready for Julian and for anybody else who had earned the privilege of

196

putting his cock inside me.

When I felt the bronze chalice we'd chosen for a communion cup press to my sex I cried out, unable to hold it back, or my pee, which came on the instant, splashing into the cup and running out over the altar to wet the skin of my bottom and back. The chant grew louder as Darius held the cup high, put it to his lips and drank. I felt my body jerk again, a response completely beyond my control, close to orgasm and yet I hadn't even touched myself.

Darius's voice was a roar as he gave the cup to Julian, who drank deeply and passed it on to the nearest of the inner circle. Another spasm ran through my body, and another, as each of our acolytes took a sip of my pee. I realised I was going to come, and would have screamed had not Darius blocked my mouth with the bulk of his erect cock. He'd pushed deep, right into my throat, but that was what I wanted, and more. I sucked hard, gagging on the head of his penis and, revelling in my own pain, grabbed his balls and squeezed hard as my teeth found the meat of his shaft.

He pulled back, to leave me snapping and clutching at his cock, my vision swimming, then suddenly clear as I saw Julian sink down and accept Darius's erection in his mouth. I screamed and I was coming, my back arched tight and my limbs kicking on the altar top as spasm after spasm of ecstasy ran through me. Julian pulled back from Darius's cock, glancing at me with concern and surprise. I didn't care, lost in ecstasy but still incomplete and knowing exactly what I needed, his cock in my body, while a tiny, terrified portion of my mind that had remained clear was screaming at me that the ritual had worked, only it wasn't Julian who was possessed, but me.

Another scream broke from my lips as I begged him to fuck me, my feet still drumming on the altar and my thighs spread wide in my need. He came close, pressing his cock to my sex, and in, driving my wild climax higher still as his

197

erection filled me. My arms went around him and I was clawing at his back as he pushed into me, spitting and hissing and I urged him to fuck me harder and faster, for all that his cock was already jamming in so deep it hurt.

I didn't care. My thighs came up to lock his body onto mine and, as he thrust into me with every ounce of power in his body, I saw the shadows closing in around me. A male hand locked in my hair, maybe Darius's, and a massive erection was thrust deep into my mouth, turning my screams to choking gulps. Something warm and wet splashed my arm and the side of one breast, another man's come, even as the cock in my mouth ejaculated down my throat. Julian's grip tightened as he rammed his cock in harder still and he'd come inside me, but it was far from over. Another man took me, twisting my body around on the altar to push himself up me from behind and slapping at my bottom as he fucked me. Yet another entered my mouth, his hand twisted in my hair as he began to fuck my throat. The man in my cunt pulled free, only to jam himself back in up my bottom hole and I was being buggered as I sucked, my body rocking back and forth on the cocks in my mouth and anus.

Now I was on my knees I could see what was going on all around me, figures jerking in the orange candlelight, men and women, using each other indiscriminately, each desperate for their own need, mouths full of cock, cunt and bottom holes penetrated, sweat-slick flesh and dark shadows moving in weird, erotic patterns. One man came close, jerking at his cock to spray come over my back and down one breast. The cock in my mouth was jammed deeper still, but only for a moment before he pulled out to finish himself off in my face and hair, until I grabbed hold of his slippery shaft and took him in once more to swallow down what he had left to give me.

Spent, he stepped away, leaving me with my mouth wide in anticipation of a new cock to suck on as my buggering continued, only for my eager gape to turn to a scream. I could now see down the path towards the Hall, along which a huge dog was lopping slowly towards me, eyes glowing like coals in the great black head, glowing red. It was coming right at me and suddenly my head was completely clear but for stark terror. I struggled to break away, still gripped by the hips as the man in my bumhole continued to thrust into me, swearing and cursing as he buggered me but utterly oblivious to what was coming. Again I screamed, yelling at him to let go and wrenching at the stone of the altar top, and as he finished himself off inside me with a grunt I shot forward, to roll off and land hard on the ground, right in the path of the hound as it entered the folly.

Panic hit me and I was desperately trying to scrabble away from the horror, crawling on the hard stone of the floor, screaming the name of Black Shuck, but the others seemed oblivious, still sucking and fucking all around me. One man squatted down to thrust his cock at my mouth, blocking my path, and the next instant I was caught, mounted, gripped by the waist and entered, my cunt filling with cock even as a man screamed and, at last, they'd realised what was happening. Darius cursed, his bass voice raised in astonishment as he saw the apparition. Other people began to scream, the cock slipped from my hole and I was free, lurching to my feet and into Julian's arms, which had never been more welcome.

He spoke to me, calm and soothing, without a trace of fear, before lifting me and carrying me from the folly and down among the reeds. Only then did I realise that he had a torch, already on as he slung me over his shoulder and started off down the path. I could see back, to the chaos around the folly, no longer brightly lit, but with faint orange light from the remaining candles flickering on the backs of a last few naked figures as they fled wildly into the woods or towards the Hall. On the altar stood Black

Shuck, his forelegs braced wide, his red eyes glowing into mine, and at that I fainted, my last thought that I had paid the price of sin.

Chapter Sixteen

THAT WAS ALSO MY first thought when I woke up, but my sudden, startled panic lasted only an instant before I realised that I wasn't in the folly at all, or anywhere near it, but on a bunk in a light, airy cabin that could only belong to a boat. It did, a big motor cruiser with a covered cabin, pushing gently through the waves to create a slight buffeting motion. I could see Julian through the door, standing at the wheel of the boat in nothing but tatty cut-down jeans and a pair of deck shoes. He was smiling, and behind him was open sky, clear blue but for a streak of high cloud.

As I threw my legs off the bunk he raised a hand in casual salute. I got to my feet, climbing from the cabin to find that we were at sea, with the coast already indistinct in the distance and the sun high in the sky. Julian gave me a happy grin, put his arm around my shoulders and kissed the top of my head, at which I started to babble questions at him.

'What's happening? What happened last night?! Black Shuck ...'

'Hush. It was a dog. Just a dog.'

'It was vast, and it's eyes!'

'Reflected candlelight.'

'No. They were glowing, and before that. I've never felt that way, when we all ...'

I trailed off, wanting to tell him that I'd felt I was possessed, but I knew he'd only make light of my experience. He'd begun to stroke my hair as he went on.

'You just let yourself go, that's all, and it really was only a dog.'

'Whose dog?'

'I don't know, but it doesn't matter. Now hush, darling, you're OK.'

'Yes, but ...'

I broke off, too confused to know what to say. Julian was always so calm, so sure of himself, but I knew what I'd seen, or I thought I did. What had happened even fitted the legend, because he'd stayed calm and it hadn't followed, while I'd panicked, tried to escape and paid the price. Yet Julian was right. I was OK – just a little sore. I was also on a boat somewhere off the Norfolk coast, which didn't make sense at all.

'What's going on?'

He stayed silent for a long time before speaking.

'I probably owe you an explanation, and an apology.'

'Why? What have you done?'

'I'd better start at the beginning. Do you remember Amanda?'

'The girl you had in the chapel? Of course.'

'And I told you that I did it to get even with Haines? Well, that was only part of the reason. Amanda was the verger's daughter, and being with her enabled me to borrow the key to the crypt and get it copied. In the crypt there was a solid silver, Queen Anne communion service.'

'You stole it!'

'No, but I was planning to. After what happened it seemed too risky, and besides, I couldn't find a buyer and it would have been a real crime to melt something like that down. I did make a few contacts though, which led on to better things, much better things, the latest of which you have become involved in.'

I didn't answer immediately, trying to put my muddled thoughts into order as I watched the coast slip away, with the implications of what he was saying sinking in only slowly. Finally Julian voiced my own thoughts.

'I'm a thief. A highly specialised art thief, but still a thief. I work on commission for wealthy collectors. Do you remember the paintings I took so much care to put into storage? They're in the bow cuddy: a Constable, a Gainsborough, a Rossetti and a beautiful Fragonard I'd keep for myself if my client wasn't offering quite so much.'

'But Vanessa ...'

'Wouldn't know a Rossetti from a risotto. Henry would, but you know what he's like. What a pair, eh? Oh, and didn't I tell you I'd even things up between you and Vanessa?'

'Thank you, I suppose. But where are we going?'

'The Baltic Coast, near Kaliningrad.'

'Russia!'

'Well, yes. My client is Russian.'

There didn't seem to be much to say to that and I went quiet again, more confused than ever, until a single thought managed to force itself to the fore.

'Why didn't you tell me?'

'I couldn't. I didn't know how you'd react, and anyway, I doubt you'd have played your part as well if you'd known the truth.'

'Played my part?'

'Yes, and you were brilliant. I'd never have managed to get so many people coming to the Hall without you, and that was essential, to say nothing of the £10,000 those idiots paid last night.'

I was smiling despite myself as he went on.

'That was very useful. Cards can be traced so it helps to have a bit of spending money. As for the way you got rid of the Inquisitor, superb! Of course he was both a blessing and a curse, because while he was a great help getting things going I couldn't have him lurking about with his camera last night.'

'Yes, but why get things going at all? Why the rituals? Why all the pretence? Why not just break in and pinch the paintings?'

'For fun, partly, but mainly because I don't intend to get caught. If I have a fault it's that I tend to be a trifle theatrical, but think about the situation. When Vanessa and Henry get back all they'll discover is that we're gone. That's why I needed the crowds, you see – to find an excuse to put the paintings into storage. It might be weeks before they notice anything's gone, maybe months, and even longer before they realise exactly what's missing, if they do at all. Then they'll call the police in and start an investigation. We'll be suspects, but not the only ones ...'

'But surely they'll realise it was us?'

'Not at all. I left a note for Vanessa, explaining that you couldn't cope with what was being done to you sexually and that we'd decided to leave without any fuss. That will make sense to her, and it will certainly make sense to the police. With luck it might even make her think twice about calling the police in at all. Then there are the 27 people who were at the ritual, most of whom are pretty keen to keep their identities secret. Remember that they include academics, wealthy eccentrics, even Satanists, which is sure to keep the police busy. There's nothing they like better than to pin the suspicion on an oddball, after all. They'll have Darius too, who's sure to bring out the worst in them. I feel a bit bad about that, actually. I like Darius, but I'm sure he'll cope, for all that he ran away with the rest of them when the dog turned up. Or the thief might have been a visitor, or a burglar. So yes, all in all, I'd say we have a better than 50 per cent chance of getting away scot free.'

'And then?'

'Who knows? Maybe my client will have another commission for me, or perhaps a break would be a good idea, holed up somewhere quiet for a while to watch the net and see if the Aylshams even realise they've been robbed. After that ...'

He broke off with a shrug. I didn't answer, still staring out across the sea. It was impossible to stifle my resentment for the way he'd treated me, which was cavalier to say the least, but I couldn't help but wonder why he hadn't simply left me at Candle Street Hall. For all the lies and deceit one thing seemed evident: that his feelings for me were genuine.

'I suppose I should be grateful you brought me with you?'

He looked surprised. 'Oh, I wouldn't leave you behind, Chloe. You're part of the loot.'

Saddled Up
Penny Birch

Amber Oakley is back! Determined as ever to avoid getting her bottom smacked but her own deep needs and the awkward circumstances she finds herself in trying to solve her financial difficulties mean otherwise.

Offering riding tuition to girls from wealthy families seems like a good idea, but Portia and Ophelia Crowthorne-Jones prove to have a few ideas of their own, and are soon indulging both their lesbian desires and their cruel sense of humour at Amber's expense. Will she end up as their plaything, or can she turn the tables and teach the little brats the lesson they so clearly deserve?

ISBN 9781907761843 £7.99